# Final Shot!

Just sixteen seconds to go against Carroll High. The score was tied at 63 all. Foward Clarence Reed had no problem inbounding the ball to Brian Davis, Jefferson's star center. But with Carroll using a full-court pressing defense, Davis spent nearly four seconds passing the ball off to his guard Terry Hanson.

Brian ran under the basket for one of his high-arching jumpers, but he couldn't get free. LaMont Jackson was open for a second, then was quickly well-guarded again.

Brian looked at the clock: 0:10, 0:09, 0:08, 0:07.

Suddenly he was open under the hoop and raised his hand for a pass. Terry saw him but was out of position.

The clock was winding down: 0:06, 0:05, 0:04.

"Shoot the ball!" yelled Coach Ford.

Terry faked a pass to LaMont and fell back a little. Just as the horn sounded, he leaped into the air for an eighteen-foot jump shot!

HEROES INC.

## FAST BREAKS

### Kirk Marshall

BALLANTINE BOOKS • NEW YORK

Special thanks to Steve Clark.

RLI: $\dfrac{\text{VL: 6 \& up}}{\text{IL: 6 \& up}}$

Copyright © 1989 by the Jeffrey Weiss Group, Inc.

Produced by the Jeffrey Weiss Group, Inc.
133 Fifth Avenue
New York, New York 10003

Library of Congress Catalog Card number: 88-92808

ISBN 0-345-35908-9

Manufactured in the United States of America

First Edition: June 1989

For my children,
Martha and Darrell,
a couple of great teenagers.

# ONE

Brian Davis, blond, blue-eyed, six feet eight inches tall and the sophomore center for the Paintville High Cornhuskers, turned and lofted a soft jump toward the basket fifteen feet away. The orange basketball swished through the net and fell gently into the hands of Jackie Barnes, the team's small senior playmaker and captain.

"Way to go, Davis." Jackie snapped a return chest pass to Brian, who now was standing at the top of the key. It was only a casual morning shooting practice on the day of the big game. But for Brian Davis, the team's leading scorer and one of the best high school players in Indiana, shooting a basketball was serious business.

"That's twelve in a row," added Jackie. Then the stocky senior smiled. "Only eighty-nine more and you'll break your old record."

"Fat chance," said Owen Klingfeld from the far corner of the half-court area, where he was about to shoot a ball. Distracted for a moment, Brian saw the smile on his best friend's freckled face. "Brian only breaks records at that crummy old hoop on his barn back home. Home-court advantage, right, Bri?"

Brian ignored Owen's remark and adjusted the ball in his oversized hands. Then, using perfect shooting form and just the right amount of backspin, he launched another high-arching jumper toward the basket. His shot arrived at the same time as Owen's and knocked his teammate's ball away just as it was about to fall into the basket. Brian's ball bounced off the clear plexiglass backboard, then swished down through the hoop.

"Dork," said Owen, smiling as he ran after his ball. The short-haired forward and Brian had been best friends ever since they played on the same biddy basketball team in the second grade. "Lucky shot," added Owen.

"Naw," said Jackie, retrieving Brian's ball and passing it back to him. "He's got the touch. Only the good shooters get those soft bounces, not klutzes like you, Klingfeld."

"Speak for yourself," said Owen.

Brian grinned and bounced his basketball a couple of times on the shiny wood floor. Except for six players shooting at each main basket and their coach standing at midcourt, the big Cobleville gym was empty. The uneven patter of a dozen balls bouncing on the court echoed in the rafters overhead, and the hollow sound made the gym seem kind of strange and lonely.

But despite the empty bleachers, Brian couldn't think of a better place to be on a breezy Saturday morning in March than at a tournament with his teammates. The Cornhuskers of Paintville had al-

ready won three straight postseason games during
the first two weeks of Indiana's famed four-week-
long high school tournament. And that evening they
were going to play their archrivals, the Cobleville
Panthers, for the Regional Tournament championship.

A shrill blast from the coach's whistle sliced into
Brian's thoughts. Palming his basketball in one hand,
he jogged with Owen, Jackie, and his other teammates toward the jump-ball circle at midcourt. A
brief meeting, Brian knew, would end the morning
shooting session and free the players for something
almost as important as basketball for Owen: a big
team lunch at a fine Cobleville restaurant.

"Time for food," said Owen, catching up to Brian.

Jackie chuckled from behind them. "It's tournament time, Klingfeld," he said, smiling. "Where's your
incentive?"

"Heck, the more games we win in the tournament,
the more free lunches Coach Tubbs has to buy us.
Now that's what I call incentive, Barnes."

As he loped toward midcourt, Brian saw a photographer from the *Cobleville Journal* step into the
gym through one of the big doors and aim his
camera at him. The sudden flash of the strobe light
blinded Brian momentarily.

"There he is folks, Brian Davis, teenage superstar,
posing for yet another snapshot by his adoring
press," Owen shouted, playfully elbowing Brian in
the ribs.

"Eat your hearts out, boys," said Brian, trying to
hide his embarrassment. At times he wished he
wasn't the center of attention all the time, but at six
eight it was difficult to hide.

At sixteen and only a sophomore, he already was

considered a star player by many of the basketball experts in Indiana. And with his height and the feathery touch on his long jump shots, Brian knew he was the reason the Paintville fans thought the 'Huskers were going to win their first regional championship in forty years.

Yet as he and his teammates gathered around their old potbellied coach, Horace Tubbs, Brian recalled the advice his dad often gave him in times of trouble: Focus on what you are trying to do and the problem will take care of itself. So he toweled the sweat from his face and forced himself to think about beating Cobleville that evening.

"Well, boys," began Coach Tubbs. He spoke around the chaw of chewing tobacco in his mouth. Brian and the others shuffled their feet impatiently as the coach spat some tobacco juice into the Styrofoam cup he held in one hand. "We've waited a long time to get to this game. Now we gotta take advantage of it. Not everybody gets a chance to win the regional."

Horace Tubbs had been the Paintville coach for twenty-five years. It seemed that almost everybody in town had either played for the "good old boy" or had relatives who had. Yet he appeared to be anything but a living legend as he stood before Brian and the others. He was dressed in scruffy old work clothes and a red-and-black hunter's cap. He'd left his boots, crusted with early March mud, at the door of the office.

"Now Cobleville has some speed, and that Morrison fella can really shoot the ball from the outside," continued Coach Tubbs. As if for emphasis, he spat more tobacco juice into the cup. "We'll have to play our best game of the season tonight if we're going to win that trophy." The coach adjusted his hunter's cap and looked out at the faces of his players, pausing for a moment when he came to Brian. "And you all know how much our town folk want this championship."

Coach Tubbs looked at Jackie Barnes. "It'll be your job to stop Morrison. Get right inside his jock and keep him from getting off so many three-point shots. He thinks he's a star, so after a while he'll probably get pretty upset and start forcing his shots." Coach Tubbs spat again. "As for the rest of their team, you other guys just stay with 'em and play your best man-to-man.

"On offense," continued the coach, rubbing his free hand across his big belly, "you all know what to do." Everybody glanced at Brian, and he felt the flush of embarrassment return to his cheeks. "Brian, their center, Addison, is a little guy. I think he's only six two. But he's got quick hands. Still, if we get you the ball down low, you shouldn't have any trouble shooting over him."

Brian nodded, then glanced at his teammates. Except for Jackie and Owen, he knew the other team members weren't especially talented. He also knew they were expecting him to lead them to victory, and he felt a nervous pang in his stomach.

After several more remarks about the strategy for that evening's game, Coach Tubbs stuck out his hand and Brian and his teammates slapped their hands on top of their coach's. They formed a tight huddle, their heads together and almost touching.

"Okay, boys," said the coach, "play hard, and play for Paintville."

"Let's kick some butt tonight," said Jackie Barnes. The other players yelled and nodded their heads.

"Okay," said Tubbs, "one, two, three!"

The players responded with a loud, "Let's go!", and they raised their hands together, breaking the huddle and ending the practice session on a spirited note.

"Don't forget," Coach Tubbs called after the players as they headed for the locker room, "we'll all be eating at the Essex House restaurant in an hour. I saw most of your parents waiting for ya in the parking lot outside. Don't be late for lunch."

As Brian and the other players walked toward the locker room door, Owen shook his head. "Don't be late? Who does coach think he's talking to. Have you guys ever seen me miss a meal?"

The others laughed, and shoved him ahead.


After changing clothes in the locker room, Brian and his teammates burst through the doors leading to the wide parking lot outside the gym. Brian, towering over the others, pulled up the collar of his green-and-gold letter jacket to ward off the chill and squinted into the stiff March breeze.

He glanced at the barren cornfields surrounding the Cobleville High School building and at the rolling hills leading toward Paintville ten miles away. It was a peaceful and familiar scene, one that always made him feel good inside.

Owen nudged Brian. "There's your mom's car," he said, pointing. Then his freckled face wrinkled with concern. "Heck, I don't see my dad's truck anywhere. He's probably still at the feed store back home."

"Come on," said Brian. Like the others, he was carrying a green-and-gold equipment bag. "We'll give you a ride to the restaurant."

Jackie Barnes laughed. "Yeah, we wouldn't want you to miss your midday feeing."

As several other players chuckled, Brian spotted the reporter from the *Cobleville Journal* who had snapped the photograph in the gym. The tall, thin man with glasses had his camera dangling from a strap around his neck and was holding a notepad. He began to walk toward the players.

"Looks like the press has caught up with you, Davis," said Owen. "Don't forget to spell my name right."

"Brian Davis?" said the man. Brian saw that he was middle-aged and had long, graying hair that blew in the wind. "I'm Paul Towson from the *Cobleville Journal*. I'd like to ask you a few questions about tonight's championship game."

Barnes waved at Brian and began to pull Owen across the parking lot. "We'll see you down at the restaurant. And don't worry about Klingfeld. I'll drive him myself."

"In your pickup?" said Owen, trying to look horrified but smiling nonetheless. "Hurry up and save me, Brian. Have you seen the old piece of junk Barnes calls a truck these days? I'm risking my life just getting into that museum piece."

"Good kids," said Towson, smiling as Owen and Jackie climbed into a battered and rusting Ford pickup, then drove away. "Like all you kids from Paintville."

"Well," said Brian, shifting his weight and feeling as uncomfortable as ever about interviews, "I guess we're just having ourselves a good time playing ball."

"Brian," began Towson, his pen poised on his notepad as he stared up at Brian's face, "your jump shot is the prettiest I've seen in all the years I've been watching high school basketball. Prettier even than Rick Mount's, and his jumper was a thing of beauty, ya know. Where did you learn to shoot a ball like that?"

Brian shrugged. "I guess the ability to play ball came from my dad. He played for Paintville years ago." The words came hard for Brian. He was quiet by nature, and interviews were difficult. "And I just practice a lot back home."

After another five minutes of questions about Paintville's team and its chances that night, Towson thanked Brian and turned his attention to Coach Tubbs, who had just left the gym. Glad to leave the questions behind and feeling good about the upcoming game, Brian strode to where his mom was standing near their old Plymouth station wagon on the far side of the lot.

But from the moment Brian spotted his mom's tear-streaked face, he knew something was wrong, and his happiness disappeared suddenly. He stared at his mother, a small, pretty woman who now seemed even smaller as she stood there sobbing. Brian stepped over to where she was dabbing at her eyes with a handkerchief.

"Mom," he said, putting down his bag, "what's wrong?"

Mrs. Helen Davis sniffled. "It's . . . it's your dad."

Brian sucked in his breath as though he had been hit in the stomach by a rebounder's elbow. "Not again. I thought he was doing better." His dad was an alcoholic, and his drinking had become worse over the past six months. Brian reached out and gently grasped his mom's shoulders. "What happened? Where is he?"

His mom wiped away a tear and looked up into

Brian's face. "I didn't want this to happen now, not on the day of your big game." Her voice was cracking. "But . . . I can't take it anymore, Brian."

"The game's not important, Mom."

His mom grabbed his arm tightly. "Yes, Brian. Yes it is. You've been blessed with a talent for basketball, and you have to use it to better yourself, to make something of yourself."

"But, Dad . . . ?"

She shook her head. "You of all people know how hard I've tried to help your father, how hard all of us have tried for two years since his store closed. Selling farm equipment was that poor man's whole life—that and your basketball." His mom blew her nose. "But his drinking is destroying all of us."

Then Brian's mother told him how she had planned to each lunch at Cobleville with Brian and his teammates, and that she had invited his dad to come along. But when it came time to drive to Cobleville, she couldn't find him anywhere. Fearing the worst, she looked in all of his favorite drinking spots, until she found him at the old Paintville rock quarry. His pickup was smashed into a tree. But he was unhurt.

She finally looked up at Brian again and completed her sad tale. "So when this school year finishes, you and I are leaving Paintville and moving to Indianapolis to live with my sister," she said, sniffling.

"But, Mom, Paintville is our home. I've never lived anywhere else. We just can't move away."

His mom seemed under control now as she put her hankie in her purse. "We can, and we will," she said, suddenly determined. "We have no family here, and it'll be best for everybody, including your father.

Maybe once we're gone he'll realize what his drinking has done to this family."

Then, before Brian could say another word, Coach Tubbs waddled over to where they were drying their tears, and Brian saw the concern on the old coach's face. Mrs. Davis apologized for their having to miss the team lunch because of the accident, then got into the car with Brian and left.


Brian spent the rest of the afternoon at home, feeling about as down as he had ever felt. By the time he was ready to leave for the Cobleville gym and the championship game, he felt drained. His mom drove him to the gym in silence, neither of them feeling much like talking.

Finally the car stopped near the locker room door and Brian got out. He bent down and looked at his mom, who was smiling at him from behind the steering wheel. "Don't worry, son, everything will work out for the best. Right now, you just go in there and win that championship for all the folks who are counting on you. I know you can do it, and I'll be there cheering as usual."

Brian nodded. "Thanks, Mom, I'll try."

And as his mother drove away to park the car, he turned and trudged toward the locker room. Playing a basketball game was suddenly the last thing Brian Davis felt like doing on that chilly March evening.


As happens in most small towns, word of Brian's family problems had already spread around Paintville and reached his teammates before they began arriving in the locker room. Feeling the stares of the other players, but not returning their glances, Brian changed into his green game uniform. He knew Owen and Jackie and the others were giving him some space to work things out himself.

Brian kept thinking about his dad's advice: Focus on the task at hand and forget everything else. And after several minutes, Brian's hurt and anger began to leave him. He nodded to himself and decided to concentrate on the game, to play the best game of his life as his dad would have expected.

Brian stood in front of his locker and looked at his teammates. "We got us a championship to win. Let's do it!"

"All right!" said Owen, stepping over to Brian and patting him on the back. "We're with you, Brian."

"Yeah," said Jackie, "let's kick some butt!"

As he ran with the team onto the brightly lighted court amidst a chorus of cheers, Brian noticed the bleachers were jammed to the back rows with wildly screaming fans from both towns. A small army of sportswriters, both local and some from Indianapolis was seated behind a long courtside press table. And the cheerleaders from both schools were jumping and waving pom-poms on either side of the floor, trying to get their cheering sections to scream even more loudly.

The game began with both teams making silly mistakes and shooting poorly. Owen fumbled the ball out-of-bounds, and Jackie threw a wild pass. For Cobleville, their star guard, Terry Morrison, traveled twice. Everyone was nervous and scared—except for Brian. Despite being closely guarded by two, and sometimes three, Cobleville defenders, he made nine of eleven jump shots and scored twenty-two points in the first half. He also pulled down ten rebounds, twice as many as anybody else, and helped Paintville grab a 41–33 lead at half time.

But the second half was a different story.

The Cobleville defenders started making it hard for Owen and Jackie to pass the ball to Brian. And when Jackie fouled out in the third quarter, the Paintville reserves couldn't guard Cobleville sharp-shooter Morrison, and he began hitting his long jumpers. At one point in the middle of the fourth quarter, he hit five three-point shots in a row.

Despite the greatest game of Brian's career so far, in which he scored a regional record thirty-seven points and grabbed sixteen rebounds, Cobleville defeated the 'Huskers 75–64. The Paintville reserves were just too inexperienced to stop the older and better Cobleville players. At the end of the game, the Cobleville fans screamed with joy and swarmed onto the court, mobbing their players.

Brian and his teammates just walked glumly back to their locker room. The season was over for the 'Huskers, but several sportswriters wanted to talk with Brian about his great game. One writer from Indianapolis even called his performance the great-est one-man effort he had ever seen in a high school basketball game.

Although Cobleville was the regional champion, Brian was named the tournament's Most Valuable Player. Exhausted, Brian trudged back onto the court and received a big trophy—along with an ovation from the fans and a kiss from his mom.

April, Brian was named to the third team, all-state all-star squad. His photograph was in all the state's major newspapers, and he was recognized as one of

Indiana's top fifteen high school basketball players. Only his continuing family problems lessened the joy of the award.

School finally ended, and Brian helped his mom pack the things they were going to be bringing with them to Indianapolis. His dad visited them twice during June before he moved to Oklahoma to live with Brian's uncle Stan and straighten out his drinking problem.

By the first of July, the old farm house was put up for sale. Brian invited Owen to play one last basketball game at the old hoop fastened to the barn wall. Then he removed the rusty rim and presented it to his best friend as a memento of their friendship.

"Just what I always wanted," Owen said, smiling but obviously affected by Brian's gesture.

Brian tried to smile, offering his hand to his friend. Owen gave Brian a bear hug.

On the Fourth of July, Brian and his mom finished packing everything into their battered Plymouth wagon and invited a dozen of their closest friends to a farewell potluck supper at the old homestead. Besides shaking hands with his mom's friends, Brian said final good-byes to Coach Tubbs and Owen and Jackie. By the time they had said all their farewells and Brian and his mom were in the car ready to leave, night had begun to fall over the cornfields.

They left their friends waving in the semi-darkness and headed for the road leading to Indianapolis. And as he thought about what strange and scary adventures awaited him in the big city, Brian felt more nervous than he had before the regional finals in Cobleville.

Within half an hour, they found themselves on the busy interstate highway leading to downtown Indianapolis. Brian looked out the window, and even in the darkness he saw the white-topped Hoosier Dome football stadium, looking like a giant mushroom among all the lighted skyscrapers. He usually traveled from Paintville to Indianapolis several times a year with his family. But now as he approached the Indiana capital with the idea of living there, the big city suddenly seemed bigger than ever.

After another ten minutes of driving, down exit ramps and through the narrow streets of his aunt Margaret's darkened neighborhood, Brian watched as his mother stopped the station wagon in front of his aunt's two-story wood-frame house.

"Look, Brian," said his mom, shutting off the engine and pointing toward the house, "it's your aunt Margaret."

And as his mother left the car and hugged his aunt, a larger version of his mom but with graying hair, Brian opened his door and got out. Immediately the smell of exhaust fumes mixing with other smells told him he definitely wasn't in Paintville.

"Hi, Brian," said his aunt. "Welcome to your new home."

After helping his mother and his aunt lug the suitcases and boxes of things from Paintville into the house, Brian saw his new bedroom on the second floor. It was roomy and pleasant with an extra-long bed and a large desk where he could do his homework. A big curtained window overlooked the street, but the glare from a nearby street lamp brightened the room even at night.

"It's all yours, Brian," said his mom, kissing him on the cheek. "You can fix it up later with your basketball posters and trophies."

Later on, Brian put on his pajamas and climbed

into the big bed. He was exhausted from the strain of the past several months and was hoping for a good night's sleep for the first time in a long while. But after the peace and quiet of the Paintville cornfields, he soon found the sirens, car horns, and noisy bus engines of Indianapolis made sleep almost impossible.

Welcome to the city, he thought, and covered his head with his pillow.

# TWO

"Good morning, Brian," said his aunt the next day at breakfast. "How did you sleep in your new bed?" She was flipping some pancakes in a skillet. Brian didn't want to worry her by complaining about the noise.

"Real good," he said, smiling as he eased his long body into a chair. His knees hit a table leg and almost spilled the orange juice. "It's not like Paintville, that's for sure."

"I should hope not," said his mother, walking into the kitchen. She was wearing a smart-looking beige pantsuit, and her hair was done up in a pretty way. "We're city folks now, so we better get used to everything, including all those sirens."

Aunt Margaret shook her head. "Isn't it just awful? This used to be such a nice residential neighborhood. Now it's becoming as bad as those places downtown. Why even along our street, gangs of kids have been caught doing all sorts of vandalism."

"We'll get used to it," said his mom, sipping juice.

Aunt Margaret handed a plate of pancakes to Brian. "Your mom's got a job interview today," she said. "Looks like she'll be working with me at the downtown clinic as a medical secretary. Lord knows we could use another good one down there."

"What are your plans today, Brian?" asked his mom.

He poured syrup onto his pancakes and forked some into his mouth. "Beats me," he said as he chewed. "At home, I guess I'd shoot some baskets with Owen out back."

His mom exchanged a glance with Aunt Margaret. "Well," she said, smiling at him in a strange way, "Owen couldn't make it, but take a look outside at the old garage around back."

Brian was puzzled for a moment, but then he smiled. "Mom?" he said, rising from the table and almost upending it with his long legs. He took a few giant steps toward the back door and scooped up his old basketball from a nearby packing box.

He burst from the house and leaped down the back steps leading to the battered old garage. He nearly stopped in his tracks on the wide paved area just in front of the garage's two wide doors. Catching his breath, he looked up and smiled at the sight of the new basketball backboard and goal fastened to the front of the garage.

"All right!" he said, bouncing his old basketball a few times on the cracked asphalt driveway, feinting and faking as though he were in a game. Then he pump-faked once and leaped straight into the air, his long arms extended and the ball in his hands, and flicked a jump shot at the new hoop from about fifteen feet away. The ball swished through the new

cotton-cord net and bounced on the pavement be-
low. "Brian Davis for two points!"

"Well, I guess the basketball goal meets with your
approval," said Brian's mom, holding her coffee cup
and walking down the back steps with his aunt. His
mom laughed. "See what I told you about Brian and
basketball, Margaret?"

Brian stepped over to his mom and hugged her.
"Hey, don't spill coffee all over me," she said, pushing
him away. "Besides, your aunt was the one who told
the guys from Sears to put everything together
before you got here. I think she deserves something,
too."

Brian kissed his aunt on the cheek, then turned
back toward the new basketball hoop and launched
another of his high-arching jumpers. "All right!" said
Brian as the ball hit nothing but the bottom of the
white cord net. "I'm hot!" cried Brian, smiling at his
mom.

"I've got that interview in an hour, Brian," she
called out. "I'll be home for lunch."

Brian just waved without looking, and soon he
was lost in his own little world of jumpers and
lay-ups and crossover dribbles.

For the rest of the morning, Brian became so involved with his imaginary basketball games that he
lost track of time. Sweat poured from his body as the
heat of the early-July day intensified.

Just before noon, he swished a long jumper from
near the back steps and was chasing down the ball
when he spotted his mom returning from her interview. Behind her he saw a tall man wearing sun-
glasses and a short, slender black kid, his head

nearly shaven, tossing a basketball from one hand to the other.

His mom walked over to where Brian was holding his basketball. "Brian, this is Coach Tom Ford from Jefferson High, your new school," she said, gesturing toward the tall white guy. The coach smiled and extended his hand.

"Hi, Brian," he said with a smile. They shook hands and Brian noticed the coach's grip was firm. "I'm always glad to meet six-foot-eight-inch-tall students." He chuckled. "Especially all-state centers."

Brian smiled weakly and shuffled his feet as he looked at Coach Tom Ford. The coach stood about six three, had neatly trimmed brown hair, and seemed to be in his late twenties. Brian thought that was pretty young to be the basketball coach of a big Indianapolis high school.

Then he remembered what his mom had said in June after learning something about the coach and the basketball program at Jefferson High School. He had been a basketball star at both Jefferson and Purdue University, and had even had a tryout with the Boston Celtics.

"And this is Reggie Dupree," said Coach Ford, indicating the smiling black kid standing beside him. "Reggie was a starter on the Jefferson varsity this past season."

Reggie stepped forward and shook Brian's hand. "Hey, man, what's happening?" he said, shifting his basketball to his other hand. He looked at Brian from head to toe. "Man, you sure are a big dude."

"Reggie lives down the street a bit," the coach said, "and he'll be a junior this year, too. I figured you two might have something to keep you busy." He pointed at the new basketball hoop fastened to Aunt Margaret's garage.

"That's a good idea," said Brian's mom. "Coach Ford and I have some paper work to go over for your transfer to Jefferson High, so why don't you and Reggie talk about basketball for a while?"

Reggie bounced his ball on the driveway. "I let my basketball do my talking." Then he took several long strides toward the basket, grasped his ball with both hands, and soared toward the rim. Floating in midair for what seemed like an awfully long time, Reggie glided under the hoop and brought the ball back over his head for a reverse slam dunk into the basket.

Brian nodded at Reggie, who was holding his ball now and smiling at him from under the basket. "Not bad," he said. "But watch this."

Brian then walked farther down the driveway until he was about thirty-five feet from the basket. He turned and leaped straight up, at the same time launching one of his high-arching jump shots. The ball sailed through the air and swished into the basket without even touching the rim.

"Man," said Reggie, retrieving Brian's ball.

"These two will be all right together," Coach Ford said, turning and following Brian's mom toward the back door. "They speak the same language—basketball."

After his mom and Coach Ford entered the house, Brian caught his ball when Reggie tossed it back to him. Reggie walked over to him, shaking his head and smiling.

"Man," said Reggie, offering a high-five to Brian and letting out a high-pitched laugh. They slapped hands. "Great shot, the kind I always dreamed of putting up."

"Yeah, well I wish I could do one of those reverse dunks," he said, as Reggie laughed again.

And for the next half hour or so, they talked and shot baskets in the backyard. They talked about basketball and last season's Indiana high school tournament, and finally a little about Jefferson High and Brian's new neighborhood. Brian found himself liking Reggie right away, and the happy kid with the close-shaved head seemed to like Brian, too.

"Look, I've gotta go home and feed my little sister," said Reggie after a while. He shrugged. "You know, what with my mom working and everything, somebody's gotta do it. So why don't you catch some lunch, man, and then I'll come back and show you around the neighborhood. We might even play some ball with the guys down at the court."

Reggie returned about an hour later, and when Brian opened the front door he saw another boy was with him. Brian told his mom he was going to look around for a while, then grabbed his basketball and closed the door behind him.

"This is Tony Zarella," said Reggie, nodding toward the kid as the three of them began to walk along the sidewalk. "Tony'll be a junior at Jefferson, too, man. He played varsity ball last season, and he can really fill up the hoop."

Brian shook his hand, and Tony looked up and down Brian's entire six-foot-eight-inch height and smiled. "That's all Coach Ford needs is a guy your size shooting twenty-footers. Oughtta give him ulcers by Christmas vacation."

Reggie cackled, and Brian took the opportunity to look at Tony, who was also laughing. He was stocky and stood about six feet tall, with a round face and brown eyes. His long black hair was bushy, and he had tanned skin and the first five o'clock shadow Brian had ever seen on a high school kid's face. Tony's legs were thick and heavy. Brian guessed he was slow out on the court.

"Finally got us a big center," said Tony.

" 'Bout time," added Reggie.

Brian saw that both Reggie and Tony were carrying balls with "Jefferson High" stenciled on them. "What's with those basketballs?"

"Coach Ford gives each varsity player his own ball," said Tony, passing his ball around his back several times. "You gotta take it wherever you go, but be sure to hold onto it in the halls at school or Mr. Rhodes, the principal, will take it away."

"Coach wants us to think about basketball all the time," added Reggie, spinning his ball on his forefinger like one of the Harlem Globetrotters. "Besides, most of us can't afford a ball like this."

As Reggie and Tony led the way along the sidewalk toward a playground barely a few blocks away, Brian got his first tour of the neighborhood. Most of the two-story houses were similar to Aunt Margaret's, and were closely packed with small backyards and dying lawns. The streets were narrow with a lot of potholes. Several trucking and delivery businesses were nearby with their large fleets of noisy, smoky trucks.

As they approached the run down playground, he saw full-court games of five against five on the two messy, asphalt basketball courts. The chain-link fence surrounding the courts had holes in it large enough to crawl through. The ripped string nets on the rims barely slowed the balls when they passed through the hoops on a made shot. Scraps of paper, old wine bottles, and empty Coke cans lay scattered along the sidelines.

"The best dudes don't hang out here," said Reggie as he led the way through a hole in the fence. "But we still oughtta get us a good game. I see some guys who can play."

Brian followed Reggie and Tony through the fence, and when he straightened to his full height he noticed several heads turning toward him. Reggie signaled for him to follow, and they walked along the sidelines to the far court where the players were older and bigger. A few black kids waiting to play at the nearer court put their heads together, and one of them pointed at Brian as he strode past.

"The word's out on you already, homeboy," said Tony.

"Yeah, these dudes don't see too many big guys around this part of town."

Brian suddenly wished he was a lot smaller. He could just about feel the stares of a dozen or so people on his back.

As they neared the far court, Tony pointed at a large brick building several blocks away. "Jefferson High," he said. "Sort of looks like a prison, doesn't it?"

And as Brian caught a glimpse of his new school, he did have to admit it sort of resembled a prison, with the heavy-wire-mesh screens covering all the first floor windows.

As if reading his mind, Reggie said, "We still don't know if those screens are for keeping bad dudes out or students in." He let out a high-pitched laugh.

Five minutes after Brian and his two new friends arrived at the court where the older kids were playing, the game there ended. The sweaty losers, bickering among themselves, left the court while the winners stayed and awaited another team to challenge them. Reggie walked toward the winners, who were toweling off, and signaled for Brian to join him.

When Brian caught up to him, Reggie said, "We'll take two of those kids standing on the sidelines and play these dudes. Around here, your team keeps playing until it loses. But these guys are nothing. Some of those good teams downtown don't ever lose and end up playing all day long."

Reggie then introduced Brian to a tall, dark-haired white kid on the winning team named Nick Vanos, the second-string center on the previous year's Jefferson High varsity. The broad-shouldered senior shook Brian's hand but never smiled. He just stared into Brian's eyes.

Reggie said, "Brian's the new—"

"I know who he is," said Nick, cutting him off in midsentence. "Let's play," said Nick finally, turning toward his team and grabbing a ball.

Brian felt puzzled by Nick's behavior. "What's his problem?" he asked, watching as Nick ran toward the far hoop and slammed the ball down through as if he were punishing it.

"Don't worry," said Tony, "he gets moody sometimes."

"Yeah," added Reggie. "Dude heard about you the other day from Coach Ford, like we all did. I guess he figures his playing time at center this year will be next to nothing with you going to Jefferson."

To fill their five-man team, Reggie chose a white kid from a nearby parochial school and a husky black kid who lived a few houses down from him. Both had been on the sidelines watching, but to Brian, neither looked like a basketball player.

As Brian warmed up, sinking one long jump shot after another, he caught a glimpse of Nick Vanos and the winning team at the other end of the court as they paused and watched his one-man shooting exhibition.

"Winners' ball out to start the game," said Nick Vanos, still wearing a scowl, "and we play to thirty baskets."

Reggie nodded. "Let's get it on, man."

And for the next half hour or so, Brian and his teammates, playing without their shirts, raced up and down the cracked asphalt court and tried to play as a team. Nick Vanos and his teammates were already warmed up from their earlier games and scored four straight baskets in no time. Three of the baskets were a result of defensive mistakes by the two kids Reggie had chosen to fill out their team.

"Let's kill these jerks," said Nick Vanos to the other kids on his team. "They're nothing."

For Brian, the early part of the pickup game was tough. He hadn't played full-court since the Cobleville game and his legs were rubbery on his first two jump shots. But as soon as he got his second wind, his team began to take command of the game.

With the score seven baskets for Nick Vanos's team and three for Brian's, Reggie suddenly stole a pass intended for Nick and raced the length of the court for a twisting, floating slam dunk that rattled the old rim. The black kids watching on the sidelines leaped to their feet, big smiles creasing their faces, and gave one another high-fives in appreciation of Reggie's high-flying playground move.

Reggie ran downcourt after the dunk and raised a fist. "Let's beat these guys, man," he said to Brian, who slapped Reggie's hand as he came back to play defense.

Before anybody knew it happened, Tony stole another wild pass at midcourt and dribbled like crazy toward the basket. Nick Vanos, his face twisted with anger, turned and loped after Tony. Brian raced after them, his long strides quickly closing the distance.

By the time Tony reached the basket, Nick was beside him waiting to smash the attempted shot back into the bushy-haired guard's face. But Tony must have seen Brian out of the corner of his eye. He pump-faked once, causing Nick to leap as high as he could, then dished a scoop pass to Brian as he ran down the middle of the foul lane. Brian caught the pass and in one motion dunked the ball through the hoop so hard that the backboard shook violently on top of its metal pole.

The kids on the sidelines exploded with howls of delight at the resounding slam dunk. Reggie ran up to Brian and gave him an enthusiastic high-five, then did the same to Tony for making such a great pass. Brian ran back downcourt feeling great.

From then on the game became a tough physical battle, especially under the basket during the heated rebounding action. For Brian, it was his first experience with city-style basketball. And although he hit five long jump shots and played well on the outside, he found the going hard under the hoop where he was shoved and hacked and elbowed all game long. To make matters worse, Nick Vanos, a slow, big kid but still an experienced playground player, drove around him for several easy lay-ups.

With the score twenty-five baskets for Brian's team to only nineteen for Nick's, Reggie made a spectacular behind-the-back pass to Brian, who sank an easy lay-up. As Brian turned to run back upcourt for defense, he suddenly felt Nick Vanos's elbow smash into his mouth. Stunned for a moment, Brian put a hand to his lips and felt blood pouring from a large cut.

"Hey, man, what was that for?" yelled Reggie, glaring at Nick. He ran over to Brian, who had blood flowing from between his fingers.

Nick smiled. "You know how it is," he said, looking at Brian. "There's no room for wimps under the hoop."

Two of Nick's teammates, a couple of white kids who appeared to be his best friends, laughed and slapped high-fives with him. "Way to go, Vanos," said one of them.

Reggie looked up at Brian. "You okay, man?" he asked, concern spreading across his face.

Brian nodded, and except for the blood flowing from his cut lip he felt all right. He'd been hit in the face during a game before, but never in such a dirty way. Now he looked at Nick, who was squinting up at the cloudy sky.

"Looks like rain," said Nick, picking up his basketball and walking toward the sidelines. He turned and looked back at Brian and Reggie. "Lucky for you guys, because we were just getting ready to kick your butts all over the place."

Nick's two friends laughed again, and followed him.

As Brian felt several raindrops on his hot and sweaty body, he could tell that the cut had almost stopped bleeding. He followed Reggie and Tony to the sideline and retrieved his old ball.

"Don't worry," said Tony. "Nick's a real jerk."

"You got that right," added Reggie. He started to hurry toward the street before the clouds burst and they got soaked. "He's been that way ever since his mom took off and left his old man to look after the family by himself. I remember Nick a few years ago when he used to be an all right dude."

"Nick's dad drinks a lot now," Tony said as they approached the street. Brian looked down at him and the black stubble on Tony's face made him appear older than he was. "They say he beats on Nick a lot. But still, he's got no right to smack you in the mouth the way he did."

As the rain fell harder, Brian just nodded and realized that despite Nick's nasty temperament, he and the big senior center had at least one thing in common: alcoholic fathers.

The summer thunderstorm began dumping sheets of cool rain on Indianapolis just as Brian and his two friends stepped inside a nearby Seven-Eleven store for Cokes and candy bars. They drank and ate and discussed the game, until finally the storm passed as quickly as it had appeared.

Brian, Reggie, and Tony stepped out into bright sunshine, and Brian noticed steam rising from the puddles on the street. After they began walking toward Aunt Margaret's house, Reggie smiled and turned toward Brian.

"Forget about this game today, man," said the slender black guard. "Tomorrow, Tony and I will take you downtown where the real dudes play ball. And it's a place where nobody'll take a cheap shot at you like Nick did today."

Brian saw Tony nodding. "Yeah, the Dust Bowl."

"The what?" said Brian, puzzled.

Reggie looked shocked. "Man, you never heard about the Dust Bowl? Why, it's the baddest playground around."

Tony looked up at Brian. "It's smack in the middle of the ghetto," he said, "but you'll find more good players down there than anywhere else in the city, maybe even in the state." Tony playfully hit Reggie with an elbow. "Homeboys lack an education."

"Do they let high school kids play?" asked Brian.

Reggie laughed. "Man, half the dudes down there are kids we'll be playing against during the season. The other half are guys who never made it once they got outta school. You know, strung out on drugs or in trouble with the law. But, man, they sure know how to play ball."

"Anyway," added Tony, "we got us a team in the league down there. Mostly varsity players from Jefferson High."

"We call ourselves the Jefferson Airwalkers, and we've won two outta three so far this summer." Reggie playfully elbowed Brian. "Man, all those guys gonna go crazy wanting to play against your big bones. That's how it is down there, guys challenging each other with their best moves."

# THREE

The next morning, Brian awoke rested and full of anticipation. His lip was a little swollen but okay. He got up and ate breakfast with his mom before she started her new job as a medical secretary.

"We can drive to work together," said Aunt Margaret.

"And," said his mom, "it'll be the same kind of work I did back in Paintville."

The mention of their old hometown sent a pang of sadness through Brian's chest and made him think about his dad. He got over the feeling by shooting baskets at his garage hoop after his mom and aunt left.

At a little before one o'clock, Reggie and Tony showed up, both of them holding the basketballs Coach Ford had given them. As Brian followed them to a city bus stop, Reggie told him about the Dust Bowl.

"No sense getting down there too early," said

Reggie, "since the best players don't show up until late afternoon, say four o'clock. Until then, there's games between the younger kids, mostly dudes who don't play for a team during the season. But after four, the heavy-duty action starts with guys like 'Dr. Dunk' Buford, 'Whirlybird' Charlie Yates, and Cornelius Pendergast, a.k.a. 'the Kangaroo Kid' by Dust Bowl regulars."

Brian chuckled at the various nicknames. "I guess they can all jump pretty good, eh?"

"*Real* serious."

"But that's the pro division," said Tony, fingering a small bandage on his face. Brian figured he must have cut himself trying to shave his five o'clock shadow. "We're in the college division, but it's really for guys still playing high school ball. The Jefferson Airwalkers got a game today at five o'clock against some team called the Attucks Aces, whoever they are."

"They're mostly black dudes from the west side." Reggie stepped over to the curb as a city bus roared up to their stop. "Oscar Brown plays for them, and he was the best center in town last year. Led Westside High all the way to the state semifinals last year as a junior."

"Oh, yeah, I hear he eats six-foot-eight-inch centers for dinner," said Tony, smiling as he paid his fare and followed Reggie onto the crowded bus. "If you think Nick Vanos's elbows hurt, wait till you go up against this guy."

"Thanks, guys." Brian ducked and entered the bus.

The forty-minute bus trip took them from their neighborhood on the northeast side of Indianapolis, through the central part of the city with its stately old homes, and close to the congested downtown area. For a moment, Brian saw the tall Soldiers and Sailors Monument, the famous old landmark standing in the exact center of the city. He also caught a glimpse of the Hoosier Dome and Market Square Arena, where the high school basketball finals were held every year. Their white domes gleamed in the sun.

Finally, they left the bus at a west-side neighborhood, and Brian immediately noticed the houses were more rundown and the streets dirtier. Small groups of black men sat on the front steps of some of the houses and small black children played among the parked cars. Most of the storefronts, many of them pawn shops or liquor stores, had heavy, metal screens covering the glass windows. As he followed Reggie and Tony for a few blocks, he noticed almost all of the people around him were black, making him feel like a minority person for the first time in his life.

They strode around a corner, and in the shadow of several tall housing-project apartment buildings Brian noticed a fenced-in asphalt basketball court nestled against an old boarded-up elementary school. Two tall metal poles with a few spotlights on top of each of them stood on each side of the court. A battered wooden scoreboard near one end of the court and a few lengths of rundown metal bleachers packed with several hundred excited fans, mostly black kids, completed the scene.

"This is it?" asked Brian. A gust of wind whipping between the tall buildings blew dust into his face, and he shielded his eyes.

"It doesn't look like much," said Reggie, blinking a little dirt from his eyes, "but now you know why they call it the Dust Bowl."

With the fans gawking at him as usual, Brian followed Reggie and Tony to a spot behind one of the battered wooden player benches on the sideline. For the next half hour or so, they watched a game while Reggie and Tony introduced Brian to some of the big playground stars. They just nodded.

As the game they were watching finished, and five o'clock rolled around, Reggie tapped Brian on the arm and pointed toward to tall black kids walking their way. Each of them stood about six three, and they both were waving to some of their friends as they entered the court area. Brian noticed that one of them wore protective goggles, and that each of them was carrying a ball with "Jefferson High" stenciled on it.

"The rest of our team," said Tony.

The two kids walked over to the bench area and Reggie introduced them to Brian. The taller of the two, the one with the goggles, was named Clarence Reed. The other, about an inch shorter, was LaMont Jackson. According to Reggie, both were going to be seniors at Jefferson, and both had been starters on last year's varsity.

"Hey, man," said Clarence, shaking Brian's hand, "we heard you was coming." Brian saw that Clarence was broad-shouldered and muscular. His goggles covered half his wide face.

LaMont, wiry with long arms, shook hands. "We're gonna need you this year, man," he said in a soft voice. He looked away, and to Brian he appeared to be sort of shy. "All we been missing the past couple of seasons was a big center who could score," added LaMont.

Then, while several young black kids reset the scoreboard and the officials took a break between games, Brian and the other Jefferson Airwalkers warmed up for their game. A small crowd gathered to watch Brian swish a dozen or so long jumpers in a row.

At the other end of the court, the Attucks Aces shot lay-ups, led by a tall muscular black kid about six feet seven. Brian figured he was Oscar Brown.

As Reggie, LaMont, Clarence, and Tony lined up around the midcourt jump-ball circle, Brian looked at Oscar Brown who was preparing for the tap-off and offered his hand to the big center. Brown, an angry-at-the-world scowl on his face, just glared at Brian without shaking his hand.

Welcome to the Dust Bowl.

From the opening tap, which Oscar Brown won easily, the Attucks Aces played freewheeling basketball. Running and jumping without letup, they shot wildly and often, missing most of their early shots. But the rebounding action under both baskets was fierce and bruising.

During the first several trips up and down the court, Brian felt Oscar Brown elbowing and shoving him. Brown knew how to use his big body and muscular arms to get the inside positions under the backboards. Still, Brian did manage to shoot well early in the game, hitting three fifteen-foot jump shots over Brown.

Brian enjoyed playing with his future Jefferson teammates, who seemed to expect a lot from him. They passed him the ball often and yelled for him to shoot his deadly jump shots, which he did until Oscar Brown began guarding him more closely.

But LaMont, with his quick catlike moves to the basket, and Reed, with his battering-ram style of rebounding, played well on their own. They were

more used to the hard-hitting city style of play than
Brian was. Even Tony, unable to keep pace with the
Aces' quick guards, managed to show off his accurate outside shot by hitting two three-pointers in the
first half. And Reggie, with half a dozen baskets, kept
the halftime score at a respectable 45–35 in favor of
the Attucks Aces.

But as Brian tired in the second half, Oscar Brown
began to show off the form that had made him the
top schoolboy center in Indianapolis last season.
Twice in a row he faked with his head, getting Brian
a bit off balance, then breezed past him for rim-
rattling slam dunks that made the fans cheer.

Early in the last quarter, after one of Brian's few
rebounds, Brown stole his long outlet pass at midcourt and began dribbling toward both his basket
and Brian, a hungry gleam in his eyes.

It was one on one, Brian against Oscar Brown.

Brian quickly got into a defensive crouch, his
weight balanced. He was determined to stop Brown
and make up for his slow performance so far.

Brown was running hard and dribbling high as he
began his drive to the basket. Suddenly, the six-
foot-seven center faked and feinted like a guard. His
tall, muscular body twisted and turned, and he
flipped a dribble pass between his legs to his other
hand.

Brian leaned one way and then the other, until he
was completely off balance, and finally fell backward onto his butt. He sprawled into the foul lane
just as Brown leaped into the air. While still airborne,
the big center spun into a three-sixty and slammed
the ball down into the basket.

The fans in the bleachers and around the chain-
link fence erupted, screaming and jumping and

slapping high-fives for nearly a full minute. The backboard-shaking dunk was the play of the game, and Brown ran back downcourt with his fist raised in triumph, his broad face aglow with excitement.

Brian had never felt more embarrassed during a game. He pulled himself to his feet and, stunned by the laughter of some fans who were pointing at him, tried to continue as best he could.

"Don't worry, man," Reggie said. "Brown's done that to a lot of dudes down here."

"You'll get back at him when we play Westside during the season," added Tony.

Brian nodded but still didn't feel any better.

The game finally ended with the Attucks Aces winning 76–68. Only Reggie's fine overall play and some rebounding and tough play under the basket by LaMont and Reed had kept Brian's team in the game. For Brian, it was the worst he had ever felt about his performance since he began playing basketball.

As both teams began leaving the court, making room for the Kangaroo Kid and Whirlybird Yates and the others in the pro division, the Attucks Aces shook hands with the Jefferson Airwalkers. Oscar Brown, smiling now, nodded at Brian, who noticed a satisfied look on the big center's face.


Following his embarrassing introduction to the rough-and-tumble city style of play, Brian spent the remainder of the summer playing basketball with his new friends from Jefferson High. He even met a couple of other future teammates at Jefferson, red-headed senior guard, Terry Hanson, and black sophomore guard, Alvin Woolridge. Both played in the remaining four summer-league games at the Dust Bowl.

"We call Hanson 'Captain Clank'," said Reggie.

Before Brian asked why, he watched the six-foot-one white senior shoot a dozen or so shots during warm-ups and saw him sink only one. The others all clanked off the rusty rim at the Dust Bowl and bounced away.

Alvin Woolridge, from the same neighborhood as LaMont and Clarence, was a skinny five-foot-eight guard who was a sharpshooter from beyond the three-point line. He also did a great impression of Michael Jackson, especially as he moonwalked across the asphalt basketball court while spinning a ball on his finger like a Harlem Globetrotter.

"Too bad Alvin don't move like that in a game," remarked Tony one day at the Dust Bowl, cracking up his teammates and causing Woolridge to take the basketball he'd been spinning and toss it at Tony's head.

As the summer drew to a close, Brian's life became long and lazy days of eating and sleeping and playing basketball on courts around the city. Then somebody mentioned that school began in only a week. And so did basketball training.

# FOUR

On the day classes began at Jefferson High, the next to last day of August, Brian's mom stopped him as he was leaving and looked him over from head to foot.

"What a handsome kid," she said, winking at him. "But stand up straight and keep your shoulders back. Be proud of your height, as well as your good looks."

His aunt Margaret laughed. "He'll drive all the pretty girls wild."

"Mom, Reggie and Tony are waiting for me out front," said Brian, blushing and shaking his head. He kissed his mom and his aunt, then opened the door. "I gotta go."

With butterflies dancing in his stomach, Brian joined his friends for the short walk to school. Even though he knew most of the varsity basketball players from his summer games, Brian figured a thousand or so kids would still be new to him. And when you're six feet eight, you sort of stick out, especially when your arrival in town has been written about in the Indianapolis sports pages.

"Don't worry about a thing," Reggie told him as they approached the school's front entrance. "Just stay close to me."

"Yeah, stay with Reggie and you'll do *real* well," said Tony, smirking.

"Hey, man," said Reggie, pointing at himself with his thumb, "everybody knows this dude."

Tony laughed. "Especially the teachers in charge of the detention hall."

But his friends couldn't ease the fears Brian had about his first day at Jefferson High. Everything was so different from Paintville. All the kids seemed to be staring at him as he entered the building.

"See you at the basketball meeting after school," said Tony.

"Yeah, man," added Reggie, "today we start physical conditioning, also known as Coach Ford's hell on earth."

After his friends left, Brian tried to find his new homeroom. He edged his way down a long, crowded hallway and couldn't help noticing how old and rundown the building was. Its woodwork was faded, many of the old plaster walls were cracked, and the gray metal lockers in the hallways were dented and scratched.

When Brian finally reached his already crowded homeroom, he was welcomed by a tall, smiling man with thick black-rimmed glasses. "Well, being as tall as you are, you must be Brian Davis," said the middle-aged man, pumping Brian's hand. "I'm Mr. Bandiwell, and I speak for all Jefferson basketball fans when I say we are delighted to have you at our school. It's been a long time since we've had an all-star center around here."

"Thanks," said Brian, a bit taken aback. "I'll do my best here."

Brian blushed slightly, and when the tone rang signaling the beginning of homeroom period, he was happy to find himself assigned to a cramped desk beside a pretty blond girl. As Mr. Bandiwell assigned the seats by calling roll, Brian learned her name was Lori Harper. And while class schedules were being handed out, he was a bit surprised when she leaned over and tapped him on the arm.

"Hi, I'm Lori," she said softly.

Brian, never too smooth with girls, swallowed and nodded.

"You're from a country town, aren't you?" asked Lori. "I mean, that isn't anything to be ashamed of." She seemed to sense his embarrassment, so she added quickly, "I . . . I came here from a small town last year, so I know what you must be feeling. I mean, with such a big school and everything."

"Thanks. It's pretty weird."

"It took me a while to stop feeling like a farm girl," Lori said, running a hand through her long blond hair. "But I like it here. Jefferson is an okay school."

Now she seemed embarrassed and looked at the papers on his desk. "Let me see your class schedule," she added. "Maybe we're in the same classes. Anyway, I guess I'll see you a lot during basketball season. I'm a cheerleader."

"You are?" said Brian stupidly. "I . . . I play basketball."

Lori giggled softly. "I know."

As Lori helped him look over his schedule, Brian tried to stop blushing and thought suddenly that

attending Jefferson High School wasn't going to be
so bad after all.

The rest of the first day of school was taken up by
classes and more hearty welcomes from Brian's
teachers and some of the other kids. Lori Harper was
in only one of Brian's classes—English. But from the
moment Miss Pinchot, the gray-haired narrow-faced
teacher began speaking about all the hard work they
were going to do in her class, he knew he was going
to need somebody's help.

"And that goes for varsity athletes, too," said Miss
Pinchot in a nasal voice. She stared at Brian, making
him squirm. "Varsity athletes should have just the
same amount of work as regular students, perhaps
even more."

After school, as Brian was walking with Reggie and
Tony to the first basketball meeting of the year, he
mentioned Miss Pinchot.

"Man, you got Pinchot?" said Reggie. "Well, I hope
you like to read. I hear she really likes to lay on the
homework."

"Yeah, like three books each grading period,"
added Tony. "What does old 'Pinchy' expect us to do
during the basketball season, read while we're waiting our turn in line for lay-ups?"

Near the door leading to the gym Brian saw an
elderly gray-haired man walking toward them. He
was round and short, and his right hand was extended in greeting toward Brian.

"Who's this?" asked Brian.

Tony chuckled. "Mr. Rhodes, the principal. I think

he was here when they built this place sometime during the Civil War. He's okay, though. Loves basketball."

"Brian Davis," said Mr. Rhodes, shaking Brian's hand and happily looking up and down his full height. "I've already heard so much about you from Coach Ford. How was your first day at Jefferson?"

"Fine, sir," said Brian.

Mr. Rhodes chuckled. "Well, I'm looking forward to watching you play basketball this season." He leaned closer to Brian and whispered. "Between you and me, all we've needed to be a great team is a big center." He nodded and waved, then walked briskly toward the main office.

"Looks like Brian's got a friend," said Tony.

Reggie laughed. "Man, when you're six feet eight you got lots of friends."

They walked into the gym, which was stifling from the intense summer heat, and Brian saw about forty kids sitting in a section of the bleachers that had been pulled out just for the meeting. He knew the returning varsity players by the basketballs they were carrying, and immediately spotted LaMont, Clarence, redheaded Terry Hanson, and Nick Vanos.

Brian also saw Alvin Woolridge sitting with some players he hadn't met yet. As Reggie and Tony led the way to the bleachers, Alvin stopped Brian and introduced two of the guys, both juniors.

The shorter of the two players, about six feet two, was a dark-haired kid with flashing brown eyes named Cisco Vega. The other one, who stood about six three, was a studious looking guy with thick-lensed glasses named Brad Cunningham. They both shook hands with Brian.

But then Coach Ford and his two assistants

walked across the floor from their coaching offices, and the players suddenly grew quiet.

"Most of you know me," said Coach Ford, "but for the people trying out for basketball for the first time, and for those of you returning players who may have forgotten how pleasant our conditioning program can be, let me first introduce myself and my two assistants. Then we can start the torture—I mean the conditioning."

The older players groaned and shook their heads.

After saying a few things about himself, the coach introduced the varsity assistant, a heavy-set six-foot-five-inch middle-aged black man named Mel Williams, who was also one of the school's career counselors. As Coach Williams nodded at the group of players, Brian saw he had a neatly kept black-and-silver goatee on his chin as well as a sizable paunch around his gut.

Reggie tapped Brian's arm. "He's an all right dude," whispered Reggie. "Used to be a big college star at Butler University about twenty years ago."

Coach Ford then indicated a pasty-skinned red-headed man who appeared to be in his early twenties. He wore thick dark-rimmed glasses, and Brian figured he wasn't taller than five seven. The coach introduced him as Pat Young, the B-team coach and a history teacher. Several former B-team players hissed and booed playfully. Coach Young just bowed slightly in response.

"All the guys like playing for him," said Tony, leaning toward Brian. "Coach Young also scouts for the varsity and gets lots of inside information about other teams."

Coach Ford spent the next fifteen minutes talking and handing out parental permission slips and lock-

ers to the players. He said the preseason conditioning program was for both potential basketball
players and returning players who were not partici-
pating in a fall sport. He also explained what the
program was all about and why it was important to
use the two months prior to the basketball season
for getting into top shape.

Then after pausing a moment, he introduced Brian
as an all-star center who had just moved to the
Jefferson school district and asked him to stand.
Brian felt his face flush with embarrassment—
especially when Reggie and Tony led the others in a
round of applause.

As the other players headed for the locker room to
get changed for the first day's workout, Coach Ford
called Brian into his small office on one end of the
gym and handed him a basketball.

"Just like the other guys," said the coach, smiling.
"Keep it and use it for pickup games after our
workouts. No coaches are allowed in the gym, but
you'll enjoy playing with the other varsity guys."
Coach Ford shook Brian's hand. "Welcome to the
Jefferson Patriots varsity, Brian."

And as Brian walked downstairs to the locker
room carrying his ball, he smiled to himself and felt
like a true member of the team.


For the next two months, Brian and the other
basketball players spent their afternoons running
and jumping and lifting weights while the three
coaches kept track of their progress. The coaches
especially wanted Brian to build up his upper body
and to improve his jumping, so he worked extra hard
with the weights. He was so exhausted every night

for the first two weeks that he could barely stay awake to do his homework.

Brian and most of the other varsity players and veteran B-team players played spirited full-court pickup games in the gym. Brian noticed Nick Vanos was absent from the games. So was Terry Hanson, who needed to keep his part-time job until just before basketball practice officially began.

"Is today the big day?" asked his mom at breakfast.

Brian finished his second bowl of Wheaties and nodded. "The first real day of basketball practice," he said, standing and gathering his books in his long arms.

"Good luck," said his mom as he left the house.

"Piece of cake," he called back, smiling and anticipating some real basketball after two gruelling months of physical conditioning.

The school day seemed to drag on forever. As soon as the last bell rang, Brian and forty other candidates for the varsity and B-team squads rushed to the locker room beneath the main gym and changed rapidly into practice clothes. Brian soon learned that the varsity used the main gym, while the B-team candidates reported to the small physical education gym next door.

Brian got into his practice uniform as quickly as possible and began to take his basketball upstairs with him, but Reggie held him back. "Man, you won't even see a basketball at one of Coach Ford's early practices," he said, shaking his head. "For the first week it's all footwork and defensive positioning drills."

Tony walked by and said, "Yeah, and don't be in

such a hurry to get upstairs either. Just be ready to run."

"And slide, slide," added Clarence, mimicking Coach Ford's voice.

Unlike Paintville where Coach Tubbs just let the players scrimmage all the time, Coach Ford spent the first week running the twenty varsity basketball candidates through various defensive footwork drills, hand movement drills, and even some hand-eye reaction exercises. For Brian, doing the drills for the first time in his life, basketball practice suddenly became boring and difficult.

"Let's move, Brian," yelled assistant coach Mel Williams on Tuesday. "Get your butt down into a defensive position and slide your feet. Slide, slide, slide!" His deep voice rang through the gym.

On Wednesday the squad worked one-on-one. Coach Ford held a ball while a defensive player denied a pass to an offensive player who was dancing around trying to get open in the half-court area. Brian was assigned to guard LaMont, whose quick moves were just too much to handle.

"Basketball is more than just shooting a ball," said Coach Williams, looking at Brian as he walked to the end of the drill line. "You have to guard out there, too. Move your feet, Davis!"

By the end of the first week, Brian was feeling a bit down about his ability, at least on defense. On Friday, as the players were about to leave practice for the weekend, Coach Ford told them that starting Monday half of the practice time would be devoted to offense and shooting.

"All right!" said several players as they walked down to the locker room. Everyone finally seemed happy, Brian noticed, except for Nick Vanos, who had arrived at school that morning with a black eye and a cut lip.

"Finally, I'll get to touch a basketball again," said junior Cisco Vega as he showered. "I almost forgot how to shoot."

"Not me, man," said Alvin Woolridge, smiling and cranking his right arm in a shooting motion. "I'm always ready to put it up. Any time, any place."

Brian slumped in front of his locker and checked the bottom of his sneakers. "I've just about worn out a pair of basketball shoes doing all those sliding drills."

"We warned you, man," said Reggie, laughing.

Coach Ford soon began working with two groups on offensive plays. First, they worked without defensive players in order to learn the plays, then against a man-to-man defense.

Two players who had been playing with the football team joined the varsity tryouts. Two-hundred-twenty-five pound, six-foot-three-inch Jeff Burgess was an all-state football lineman as well as a returning basketball letterman. George Ross, a wiry six-two defensive back and B-team basketball player last season, was known as "Glue" because he could stick to an offensive man no matter how fast the action was.

Following the two weeks of drills as well as a brief scrimmage, during which Brian shot well but made some defensive mistakes, Coach Ford cut the squad to the final twelve-player varsity roster. Brian checked the list that was posted in the locker room and noticed that he and Nick Vanos were listed as the team's centers. Reggie, Tony, Terry Hanson, Alvin

Woolridge, and Cisco Vega were the guards. And LaMont, Clarence, Brad Cunningham, George Ross, and Jeff Burgess were the forwards.

Following a restful weekend at home shooting baskets and catching up on his homework, Brian arrived at practice on Monday to learn he had been given the varsity's starting center position over Nick and Clarence. Coach Ford announced his decision to start Brian over Vanos just after he whistled the players over to a prepractice meeting at midcourt.

"We're going to try and build our offense around Davis," the coach announced in his usual strong, positive voice. "We'd like to use his shooting ability both as a weapon and as a decoy to force the other teams to double-team him. Hopefully, that will leave the rest of you open for some easy baskets."

"And if Jackson, Dupree, and the rest of you guys keep moving on offense," added Coach Williams, "then Davis should be able to get the ball to you in the open."

After practice, the players discussed the coach's decision. Brian was used to being the whole offense at Paintville, but now Coach Ford wanted him to pass as well. He'd have to get used to it.

His teammates had plenty of suggestions.

"Man, it's no problem," said Reggie, unlacing his high-tops. "Just look for me and your worries are history."

"Yeah, you'll never see the ball again," said Tony.

The other players laughed and shook their heads.

But then Nick Vanos, the skin beneath his left eye still discolored and his lip swollen, suddenly exploded. "Damn it," he said, glaring at Brian. "I don't like this crap! If anybody deserves to be the starting center it's me! I'm a senior, and this was supposed to be my year to start." His face darkened with anger as he pointed at Brian. "Then big boy here arrived."

LaMont, as cool and under control as always, played the role of peacemaker and said calmly, "You'll still play a lot, Nick. Take it easy."

"Hell, no!" said Nick, slamming his sneakers into his metal locker and storming off toward the shower. "I been outplaying Davis for a week now. It's not fair!"

Silence filled the locker room until Reggie shrugged and said, "The boy's entitled to his opinion."

"Forget it, Brian," said Tony, dressing. "That's the way Nick is. Besides, I hear he's been having problems at home again."

That week Brian and his teammates began working together on the court. LaMont was driving to the basket, Reggie was a great playmaker, and Terry Hanson won the other starting guard spot despite his awful shooting. Brian and Clarence did most of the rebounding, with football star Jeff Burgess and Nick providing solid backup. Brian did his best to learn Coach Ford's quick-moving offensive system.

That Thursday, the trouble started.

Reggie and Tony met Brian at his aunt's house and started to walk to school. Suddenly, Reggie stopped dead in his tracks.

"Man! Will you look at that!" Reggie pointed back toward the garage.

The other boys turned to see the words: GO BACK TO

THE FARM painted in bright yellow across the wide garage doors.

"What jerks would do something like that?" Tony asked, shaking his head. "That's really lame."

"I better go tell my aunt," Brian said. "You guys go ahead. I'll catch you later."

Brian's aunt took the bad news well. Nothing seemed to rattle her. "Brian, don't you worry about the doors. Needed a new paint job anyway. Now, hurry up or you'll be late for school."

Brian made it to homeroom just before the late bell rang, but noticed a crowd around his locker outside in the hall. His heart started pounding when he saw Mr. Rhodes at the center, looking at his locker. Brian pushed closer in to see what everyone was looking at. Someone had painted GO HOME! across his locker in bright yellow paint.

# FIVE

Mr. Rhodes vowed to immediately begin an investigation into the vandalism at Brian's locker. "We've never had an incident like this before," said the grandfatherly principal to Brian, the distress evident on his round face. "We'll get to the bottom of this."

The Indianapolis police began their own investigation of the vandalism at Aunt Margaret's garage and said they hoped to have some information soon.

At practice, Reggie and Terry and LaMont and the others told Brian they couldn't think of anybody at Jefferson who could've done it.

"Man, it must have been some young neighborhood punks," said Reggie.

"Everybody at school knows we'd kick their butts if they ever did a thing like that," added Clarence.

Before practice began, Coach Ford took time to tell the team that occasional foolish acts by stupid individuals sometimes occur, but that the players shouldn't let this incident affect their performance on the court.

"Let's just concentrate on the intrasquad scrimmages coming up next week," said the coach.

Brian was feeling pretty low. All Thursday evening he sat in his room with his thoughts. He didn't feel like doing any homework, and all he could think about was the yellow paint on the garage and his locker. He wondered who could hate him so much to do such a thing, and why.

As he lay sprawled on his bed staring at his posters of Larry Bird and Magic Johnson, he also thought about the growing pressure he was feeling to be the super basketball player everybody at Jefferson High expected him to be. Many of his teachers had already told him they were hoping for a championship this season, and that he was the player they were counting on to get the job done.

When his mom brought him some cookies and hot chocolate later in the evening, she said, "Don't let this vandalism get you down, Brian. It was obviously the work of some disturbed kids who don't know what a nice person you are."

"Yeah, I guess, Mom. Thanks."

She smiled and stroked his blond hair before leaving.

But then the same disturbing thoughts wormed their way back into his mind. Letting the chocolate grow cold and not even touching the homemade cookies, he fell asleep fully dressed and dreamed about drowning in a giant lake of yellow paint.

At school the next day, the hot topic was the trashing of Brian's locker and his aunt's garage.

Wherever he walked, Brian felt even more stares than usual, and at practice his spirits were so low that he didn't feel like joining in the typical Friday afternoon craziness of his teammates.

During a brief full-court scrimmage in preparation for the following week's two intrasquad games, Brian's play was so sloppy that Coach Ford yelled at him for the first time since basketball began. The coach was especially angry after Nick Vanos, of all people, drove easily around him for a dunk shot.

"Davis, move your feet," shouted Coach Ford. "Basketball is more than just shooting long jump shots. You have to guard somebody." Then the coach added, "Nice move, Vanos."

After practice, as the other players were discussing their plans for the weekend, Brian dressed as quickly as he could and turned down an offer from Reggie to play basketball at a nearby recreation center on Saturday. All Brian wanted was to stay at home and be somebody other than Brian Davis, star basketball player.

"The season opens in one week," Coach Ford was telling the varsity at Monday's practice. "And this week we'll have two intrasquad scrimmages. First, today's game, which will be closed to the public, and then the annual Blue-White scrimmage, which I hope will be attended by most of the kids and teachers in the school."

"And today, we'll be using regular officials," added Coach Williams in his baritone voice. "It's time for you guys to start reacting to gamelike situations and to cut down on your fouls." He stroked his goatee and smiled. "Besides, I know you're all sick of *my* whistle blowing every day in practice."

"Man, you know it," said Reggie with a smile.

The players laughed. Brian tried to smile.

For the scrimmage, Coach Ford divided the squad into the White team led by Coach Williams and the Blue team handled by Coach Young, who left his B team for the day to help with the scrimmage. Coach Ford said he'd be watching both teams and making comments.

Brian was the center for the White team, along with LaMont and Brad Cunningham at the forwards. Tony and Cisco were the guards, and big Jeff Burgess was the only sub. The Blue team started Nick Vanos at center, and Clarence and the defensive specialist George Ross at forward. The guards were Reggie and Terry Hanson, with Alvin Woolridge on the bench to begin the scrimmage.

One of the two Indiana High School Association officials, wearing a striped shirt, blew his whistle, and Brian outjumped Nick at midcourt to start the scrimmage. The Whites took charge immediately with LaMont driving hard to the hoop for several early baskets and Cisco making a nice pass to Brad Cunningham for an easy lay-up. On defense, Brian blocked a lay-up attempt by George Ross and LaMont stole the ball from his buddy Clarence and raced downcourt for a rim-shaking slam dunk.

"Way to play defense, Whites," shouted Coach Ford.

But the Blues responded with three quick baskets of their own. Clarence drove around Brad as if the slow-footed forward were nailed to the floor and dunked the ball through the hoop. Reggie faked and feinted with a few "shake and bake" playground moves and laid the ball in easily while Tony was entangled in his own legs at the top of the key. And Alvin, alternating with Terry at guard from time to time, swished a long three-point shot.

As the scrimmage progressed, Brian found himself messing up the coach's offensive system with several poorly thrown passes. His usually accurate jump shots were just a little off target, and his legs felt slow and heavy. And to make matters worse, Nick Vanos won the scrimmage for the Blues by driving around the flat-footed Brian for a wide open lay-up along the baseline.

After the scrimmage, Coach Ford took Brian aside. "This was only a scrimmage, Brian, but I've seen you play a lot better." His soothing voice reminded Brian of his father's. "What's on your mind, that stupid vandalism?"

Brian shrugged. "I guess it's a combination of things, Coach," he said, toweling off. "I'll be all right once the season starts."

The coach put his arm around his star center's shoulder. "Listen, Brian. Sometimes it's tough to keep it together and still play a good game. Get dressed and meet me outside. I've got some people I want you to meet."

Brian looked puzzled but hustled into the locker room.

Fifteen minutes later, Brian was sitting in Coach Ford's old Mazda, cruising down the tree-lined streets of a nearby residential section of the city. They finally stopped in front of a medium-sized recreation center and parked.

As they ventured into the recreation center, Brian caught a glimpse of the basketball floor—and the ten men racing around it in wheelchairs playing a full-

court basketball game, complete with everything
except dribbling and running. The enthusiasm of the
men was obvious.

"Coach?" asked Brian. "What . . . ?"

"Just watch," he replied.

Brian folded his arms across his chest and wondered why his coach had brought him to see a
wheelchair basketball game. But then standing along
the sideline, he found himself becoming involved in
the fast-paced action on the court. He was amazed at
how well the disabled players could shoot a basketball from a seated position, and how they did just
about everything so-called "normal" basketball players did, except run of course.

The game ended when a dark-haired man with
muscular arms swished a thirty-foot set shot, causing Brian to grin and applaud. On the court, the
winners reacted like players everywhere and
slapped high-fives with one another in celebration.
Then the man who'd made the set shot wheeled his
chair over to where they were standing and shook
hands with Coach Ford.

"Brian," the coach said, "this is Mike Wood, who
works with the handicapped people down here at
the rec center."

They shook hands, and Brian noticed how strong
a grip he had. "Glad to meet you, Brian. I hear you're
quite a basketball player over at Jefferson High
School."

"I couldn't have shot better than you did just now."

Mike laughed and toweled some perspiration from
his face. "Well, I really enjoy the game. Before the car
accident that messed up my legs, I used to played
ball every opportunity I had. Now I get together four

times a week with this wheelchair team and prepare for tournaments all over the country. I can't seem to get enough basketball."

The other players waved to Mike and wheeled themselves out of the recreation center. Seeing the dedication and enthusiasm of these so-called disabled basketball players caused Brian to feel suddenly ashamed of the silly way he had been reacting to the pressure at school. "You guys sure don't let things get you down," Brian said.

"We all have challenges," said Mike, "but I have a secret for success I'd like to share with you." He shifted his weight in his wheelchair and looked up at Brian. "It's simple: 'Be yourself.' Just be the person you are and not what others may think you are. If us guys out here listened to others all the time, we'd never be able to play basketball. Some people believe disabled guys should stay on the sidelines cheering, not playing."

When Brian got home, he hugged his mom and aunt Margaret and rushed through his dinner. Then despite the chilly November air and the poorly lighted area near the garage, he shot baskets for an hour, swishing almost everything until he was overflowing with confidence again.

After his homework and before he slipped into bed, Brian felt more determined than ever to reach his potential as a basketball player. He took an index card and wrote the words BE YOURSELF on it with a red marker, then taped the card to his dresser mirror.

*Now*, he thought, *I'm ready to open the season.*

* * *

For the next two days, Brian was his old self at practice. He swished shot after shot, made sharp passes to teammates cutting to the basket, and even looked a little better on defense. Thoughts about yellow paint and the pressure being placed on him by the Jefferson fans faded into the back of his mind.

"Man, what's with you?" asked Reggie, smiling. "You been taking vitamins or something?"

After Brian swished a twenty-five-foot jump shot during a scrimmage, Coach Ford said, "Nice shot, but that's not where six-eight centers should be playing." But Brian just smiled and trotted back to play defense, the words "Be yourself" flashing in his mind.

During Miss Pinchot's English class, Brian even volunteered an answer about the book they were discussing. His response startled the narrow-faced old teacher into smiling and saying in her nasal voice, "That's correct, Brian. I'm glad you've finally decided to speak out and become a member of this class after only three months."

After practice that day, the coaches handed out the game uniforms. Each varsity player received a white uniform for home games and a blue uniform for away games. And to Brian's surprise, each of them got two sets of warm-ups, white for home games and blue for away—each with the player's name on a satin strip attached to the jacket with Velcro.

As Brian sat in front of his locker fingering the name "Davis" on the back of his white warm-up jacket, Coach Ford stepped out of the uniform storage locker and blew his whistle.

"If any of you need to have your uniform altered a bit," he said, "take it home tonight. But remember, tomorrow is team picture day, as well as the Blue-White scrimmage. So unless you want to play in front of the whole school in your practice stuff, remember to bring your uniform back to school and hang it in this locker area by the end of the day."

Reggie stopped at Brian's locker and laughed. "Man, look at this," he said, holding up Brian's extra large uniform shirt and pointing to the big number fifty. "We haven't had anybody big enough to use 'fifty' before."

"Yeah," said Brian, "it's so big it looks like a tent."

"Stop bragging," said Tony, trying on his number "11" uniform, which fit like a glove on his stocky body.

On the far side of the varsity locker room, Brian saw the three B-team graduates—Alvin, Cisco, and George—holding their first varsity uniforms. While nearby, LaMont and Clarence just took it all in stride, trying on their uniforms, then returning them to the locker without showing much emotion of any kind.

But for Brian, receiving a team uniform had been a big thrill from the time he got his first one as a biddy basketball player back at the Paintville elementary school. Now, as he brought his first Jefferson High uniform home for his mom to alter slightly, it was just as big a thrill.


The annual Blue-White intrasquad scrimmage was always open to the public and, according to Reggie, attracted a large crowd.

"Man, the fans will be out in force today," said

Reggie, changing into his blue road uniform. "And this boy is gonna give 'em a show to remember."

Terry Hanson, checking his red hair in a mirror, turned toward Reggie and said, "You mean you'll be showing them what an exceptional passer you are by feeding me for basket after basket? Sounds cool to me, Reg."

Tony, who was on Brian's team for the scrimmage, adjusted his white uniform and said, "Naw, Reggie'll be too busy looking for the ball after I pick him clean a few times." He laughed and pointed a finger at Reggie.

"Forget it, man," said Alvin Woolridge, straightening out some wrinkles in his blue jersey. He moon-walked back to where Tony was combing his hair in front of a mirror. "After you've been chasing me all game, Zarella, you won't have anything left to steal the ball from poor little Reggie."

The other players laughed, and even Brian, who usually avoided the locker-room chatter, found himself chuckling. And as they all walked toward the stairs leading to the gym, Brian realized the team was coming together like a family, and he was glad to be an important part of it.

But as they approached the midcourt area where a photographer had his camera on a tripod, Brian saw Nick Vanos trailing behind everybody else and he wondered why the center seemed even more upset than usual.

After five nervous minutes standing in a semicir-cle before the camera, and several minutes trying to keep Reggie and Cisco Vega from laughing all the time, the photographer finally snapped the team picture. The coaches seemed relieved. After they got out of their blue sweats, the varsity split up into the same two scrimmage teams as before and began to warm up at the two main baskets, except for Nick, who was walking toward the coach's office.

As he dribbled from spot to spot on the half-court area and released his high-arching jump shots, Brian also watched as the three-thousand-seat gym filled to about half capacity with chattering students and smiling teachers. Mr. Bandiwell, his homeroom teacher, stepped briefly onto the court to shake Brian's hand. And even Miss Pinchot waved at him as he was retrieving his ball near the seats. Mr. Rhodes, the principal, yelled some muffled encouragement as he walked out of the gym.

As Brian spent the next ten minutes working up a sweat by running in for lay-ups, he spotted Lori Harper, her long blond hair flowing halfway down the back of her red-white-and-blue cheerleader's uniform. When he knew she was looking his way, he ran toward the basket and slam-dunked the ball through the hoop with both hands.

Out of the corner of his eye, Brian saw Coach Ford signaling for both scrimmage teams to head toward the locker room for some reason. He retrieved his basketball and trotted off the court with the other players as the first basketball crowd of the season applauded.

When he arrived downstairs, Brian was as stunned as the others to see Mr. Rhodes standing near a blackboard with a nervous-looking Nick Vanos beside him. Brian was even more surprised to see a uniformed Indianapolis police officer also standing near both of them.

"All right, guys," said Coach Ford, "Mr. Rhodes would like to speak to you for a few minutes, so give him a little more attention than you usually give me."

The short gray-haired principal stepped forward and cleared his throat. "In my hand," he said in a grave tone, holding up a sheet of lined school paper, "is a signed confession from two male students here at Jefferson admitting their roles in the recent vandalism against Brian Davis's locker and his aunt's garage."

Mr. Rhodes paused, and Brian couldn't believe his ears. He waited anxiously for more details.

"Apparently," continued Rhodes, "two so-called friends of Nick Vanos were so upset at his not being named the starting center for the varsity basketball team that they decided to show their displeasure with lots of yellow paint." The principal paused again, and Brian saw Nick staring at the floor, seemingly close to tears. "I must say, however, that Nick had nothing directly to do with the actual vandalism. But I'll let him tell you all about it."

Brian watched as Nick wiped away a tear and looked up at the players for a long moment before speaking. "I . . . I'm sorry for embarrassing you guys," he said in a cracking voice, "by having this happen on the day of the scrimmage." He looked over at Brian for a moment, then continued. "And I'm sorry for what happened to Brian and to his aunt's garage. But these two guys I know said they were going to do something 'cause they figured I should have been named the starting center. But I swear I never knew what it was going to be. The day after they trashed Brian's locker, they told me. I didn't do anything about it then, and I know I should have." He paused to wipe away another tear.

The locker room was dead quiet. Brian saw that everybody was hanging on each of Nick's emotionally charged words. Mr. Rhodes then stepped in and, after patting Nick on the back, finished the big center's speech for him.

"So Nick finally came to see me this morning," said the principal, "and after that it was easy to get the written confessions from the two students involved. I assure you they'll be punished, most likely by being suspended from school for quite a spell."

The Indianapolis police officer stepped forward. "I'm here today to say that Brian Davis's aunt has decided to drop all charges against the two individuals involved, so as far as we're concerned, the case is closed."

Mr. Rhodes started to walk from the locker room. "Boys, you have a scrimmage to play in a few minutes," he told the players, "so we'll let you get ready." He stopped and faced Coach Ford. "I'll leave the rest up to you, Coach."

After the principal and the officer left, the locker room was silent until Nick said, "What I'm gonna say to you guys isn't easy for me, but I gotta say it." He seemed to have recovered a little and Brian noticed he wasn't crying any longer. It seemed as if the whole team was feeling bad for him.

"I'm sorry, Coach," continued Nick, "for not having the guts to speak up sooner." He looked at Brian. "And I didn't mean for anything bad to happen to Brian. But things haven't been too good at my house lately." He swallowed hard.

A long moment of silence followed before Coach Ford cleared his throat. "Well, I'm a little disappointed that Nick didn't come to me when all this began. But I'm also proud that he finally did the right thing." The coach paused and looked at Brian. "And since Nick has already apologized, I think I'll leave it to Brian to decide whether he feels that's sufficient to put this all behind us. After all, we have a long basketball season ahead of us."

Brian felt everybody turning to stare at him, so he looked up at Nick and nodded. "Sure," he said, knowing from experience what Nick must have been going through at home with an abusive alcoholic father. "I guess it's time we finally played this scrimmage."

"Yeah," said Reggie, "way to go, man."

And as the other players stood and shook Nick's hand, Coach Ford stepped over to the blackboard and tried to get their attention. "Listen up," shouted the coach. "Here's what I want you guys to do during the scrimmage today."

As the varsity returned to the court, the resolution of the yellow paint problem and the cheers of the huge crowd packing the Jefferson High gym caused adrenaline to pump through Brian's veins. He was even more excited when he saw his mom and aunt Margaret sitting in the bleachers, apparently having left early from work.

Coach Ford had told the players to run their offense smoothly, to work their butts off on defense, and that he wanted to see some teamwork during the scrimmage. And with the season-opening game just a week away, Brian was looking forward to playing in front of a large crowd again.

A striped-shirted official tossed up the ball between Brian and Clarence, who played forward for the Blue team but was a better leaper than Nick, and to everyone's surprise the shorter Clarence won the tap to open the game. Brian shook his head and ran down the court to play defense, immediately reaching up and blocking an attempted driving lay-up by Reggie.

"In your face," said Brian to his friend, who smiled.

Brian played better than he had since starting the practice season at Jefferson. On offense, he started the game by catching a high pass by Tony in the post area and turning around right away to shoot a ten-foot jump shot over Nick.

Coach Ford yelled to Nick, "Don't let Davis get position so close to the basket."

But the very next time the White team had the ball, Tony called out the number of a special play the coaches had designed for Brian. While Brian was playing under the basket, trying to fake Nick out of position, his teammate LaMont suddenly ran up behind the unsuspecting Nick and set a blind pick on him. Using the pick to lose Nick and to drive away from the baseline and toward the free throw line, Brian caught a sharp pass from Cisco Vega, the other White-team guard. Then he leaped straight into the air and swished a fifteen-foot jumper.

Down at the other end of the court immediately following that play, slow-footed Brad Cunningham, playing with his thick-lensed glasses, managed to knock away a pass intended for Clarence under the Blue team's basket. Brad's white-shirt teammate Cisco Vega picked up the loose basketball and, spotting Brian racing down the side of the court with only Nick trying to run back on defense, threw a perfect lob pass the entire length of the court. Brian caught the pass to the right of the basket, took two long strides away from the trailing Nick and slammed the ball down through the hoop.

The Jefferson High fans rose together and cheered

wildly, as did Brian's mom and aunt. Brian spotted Mr. Bandiwell slapping a high-five with Mr. Rhodes along the sideline.

As Brian ran downcourt to play defense, he was surprised to find Nick trotting alongside him, his hand extended. "Nice drive to the basket," said Nick, smiling at last.

Remembering the summertime elbow by Nick to his mouth but quickly pushing the thought from his mind, Brian returned the smile and slapped his hand down onto Nick's.

"Way to go, guys!" shouted Coach Ford. "Now we're looking like a team out there."

While Brian knew he lacked some offensive moves to the basket and that he still wasn't the best rebounder around, he felt the happiest he had since his arrival from Paintville several months ago.

# SIX

"Most of you played well in the scrimmage yesterday," said Coach Ford at Friday's practice. He looked lean and fit in his coaching shorts, and Brian figured the coach could still play like an all-star.

Coach Ford continued. "But we still need some work on our rebounding and our defensive footwork. I saw too many men cutting to the basket for open passes."

They were standing in a circle at midcourt.

Coach Williams stroked his goatee. "Yeah, and with the tough schedule we play, you know we'll be going against some speedsters. Even the big men we face can get a step on you if you let 'em." His broad black face brightened. "But the one thing I did like about the scrimmage was the shooting. Davis, Jackson, Hanson, even Dupree put on a real show."

"We better put everything together by Tuesday night at Carroll," Coach Ford added. "Those kids know how to play ball, even if you guys think they're just a bunch of farm boys."

A couple of players glanced at Brian.

"Farm boys are tough," he said, smiling.

Reggie laughed, and the others followed.

Coach Williams nodded. "He's right, but if you don't believe him just ask Westside. They played up at Carroll a couple of years ago and got their butts kicked."

The players grew silent, and Coach Ford nodded.

"So let's expect a tough game up at Carroll on Tuesday," he said. "It's always rough opening the season on the road, but it's really bad if you're not mentally prepared."

Clarence said, "Good, no running today, just mental exercises. Right, Coach?" Brian saw his eyes gleaming with mischief behind his protective goggles, and he smiled broadly.

A few players laughed, but Coach Ford just smiled.

"Nice try, Reed," said the coach, "but our defense against the fast break needs work, too. How many times during the scrimmage did Davis or Jackson or Dupree get downcourt for an easy lay-up? Too many times, that's how many. And the only way to stop the break is to run like crazy."

All the talk about the opening game and the scrimmage made Brian anxious to shoot a ball and run a fast break. He actually found himself looking forward to what apparently was going to be a tough practice.

"Right," said Coach Williams, checking his clipboard. "Anything else before we work these gentlemen to death?"

"A few minor items," said Coach Ford. "First, as

promised, there's practice tomorrow morning. We don't practice much on Saturdays, but with four games coming up in the next couple of weeks, we need the work. Be here at eleven."

Cisco laughed. "Hey, what about cartoons?"

"What about sleep?" asked Tony.

"From what I've seen of your grades lately, Zarella," said Coach Williams, trying not to smile, "you obviously get enough sleep in chemistry class."

The players laughed, and then Coach Ford reminded them about the pep rally on Monday before practice and said he'd be naming this year's captain sometime during the day on Monday.

"It's an important job," he said. "Some coaches hold elections, but I want a captain I feel I can trust and work with, and you don't always get one with an election. That's why I name him myself. Usually it's an experienced senior, but not always. I'll let you know on Monday."

Finally, the coach mentioned that night's dance, the famous "Harvest Romp."

"Try to be there," said Coach Ford. "I'll be there as one of the chaperones." He smiled, then continued. "If we want the kids at school to support us by coming to our games, we oughtta attend a dance now and then. And now is a better time than later in the season during tournament time."

"But remember, there's practice in the morning," added Coach Williams, heading for the sidelines to begin practice, "so get home before midnight. Now, let's do some laps."

And without any further discussion, the team ran twenty-five laps around the perimeter of the court and spent ten minutes loosening up with some flexibility exercises. Then they began the serious stuff, half of them at one end working on offense with Coach Ford and the rest working at the other end on defense with Coach Williams. They switched ends after twenty minutes. And later they ran three-man, then four-man, fast breaks for half an hour, stressing the proper way to play defense against the break when you're outnumbered. They finally finished the grueling two-hour practice with one of Coach Ford's favorite foul-shooting games.

"All right," said the coach as the players lined up around one of the foul lanes, "each player must make two consecutive free throws before he's outta here and on his way to the dance. But if you miss one, either the first shot or the second, then it's a lap around the court and a wait until your turn comes again."

Some players groaned and shook their heads.

"Piece of cake," Brian said.

LaMont was the first to shoot his two free throws, and the other players tried to distract him to make him miss. But the slender senior swished both shots, and pointed at his teammates.

"I'm cool, man. You can't rattle me."

Then Brian stepped up to the free throw line, bounced the ball several times, and calmly swished his first shot. The second shot, however, struck the front of the rim, then hit the back of the rim, and finally rolled around and almost fell out before it dropped through the basket.

"Shooter's bounce. All right!" Reggie said.

Then Reggie missed his first shot, much to the delight of LaMont and Brian who were walking toward the locker room. Reggie began his lap around the outside of the court.

Brian stayed at the top of the stairs, toweling off

and watching his teammates complete the free-throw-shooting game. As he watched, he saw Coach Ford walking over to him.

"It's lots of fun," said the coach, nodding toward the free throw line, "but I'm looking for players who can shoot 'em under pressure—like during the last few seconds of a tie ball game. You don't run laps if you miss then, but we lose the game."

Brian nodded, realizing how easy it was to talk with Coach Ford, unlike old Coach Tubbs at Paintville. "Maybe we should win by twenty," said Brian, smiling. "That way we won't have to send anybody to the line."

"Thinking big, huh?" Coach Ford chuckled.

Within a few minutes, Brian watched Tony, Alvin, and Brad swish their first two shots and run happily toward the locker room. Poor Reggie missed again and Brian could hear him swearing to himself as he rounded the court on another punishment lap. LaMont poked his head out the doorway in time to see Reggie trot past.

"Dupree, you oughtta be in shape by now," yelled LaMont.

Brian and Coach Ford laughed, and Reggie scowled.

Finally, Reggie and Clarence and George Ross made the two shots necessary to leave practice. Only Jeff Burgess, Cisco, Nick, and Terry Hanson remained standing at the foul lane, until Cisco and Nick made their shots.

The players who had just finished stood at the top of the stairs with the coach and Brian and watched the action. They began yelling playful insults at the two remaining shooters and discussing which of them they thought would be the loser. When Terry

Hanson missed the second of his two final free throws after Jeff had sunk both of his, he heard a new round of jeers from his teammates. Coach Williams gave Terry the "grand prize", a five-lap round-trip tour of the court.

"Captain Clank strikes again," yelled Tony, heading downstairs.

"Don't forget, practice tomorrow morning," Brian heard Coach Ford yell as he and his teammates leaped down the stairs to the locker room.

Brian had always avoided dances while at Paintville High, but now he felt suddenly trapped by Coach Ford's suggestion that all the players attend the Harvest Romp in the Jefferson High cafeteria. Usually comfortable in jeans, a scruffy sweatshirt, and basketball shoes, he now struggled with his tie and the ill-fitting navy-blue blazer he saved for such rare occasions, and which the coach had insisted they wear. And he wasn't too pleased when he looked himself over and saw that his slacks were an inch above his ankles and his brown penny loafers were scuffed and dull looking.

"Oh, well," he said, straightening the index card taped to his mirror, "as the man said, 'Be yourself.'"

He walked down the creaking stairs to his aunt's living room, and immediately his mom and his aunt gave him once-over motherly glances.

"Well, who's the lucky girl going to be?" asked Aunt Margaret, chuckling.

"You're not only smart," said his mom, "but you're a handsome kid as well."

"Give me a break," said Brian, feeling even more uncomfortable already.

As he put on his coat near the front door, Brian glanced at his basketball on the small table where he always left it and debated whether to bring it to the dance, but then decided against it. He said good-bye to his mom and aunt, then joined Reggie and Tony outside for the short walk to Jefferson High School. He noticed Reggie was carrying his basketball.

"This classy dude brought his basketball," said Tony, nodding toward Reggie. "Who brings a ball to a dance?"

"Man, I feel naked without my basketball," said Reggie, spinning his ball on his forefinger as he walked.

Brian laughed and hoped the evening passed quickly.

They walked through the cold late–November night and arrived within fifteen minutes at the large doors leading into the school cafeteria. After each of them paid a two-dollar entrance charge, Brian and his friends checked their coats—and Reggie's basketball—and stepped into what used to be the cafeteria. For the evening, it had been transformed into a beautifully decorated farmland scene, complete with cornstalks, pumpkins, and some borrowed small farm equipment.

"Man," said Reggie, gawking at the decorations and speaking over the loud rock music blaring from a nearby stereo, "you oughtta feel right at home, Davis."

Tony pointed at the refreshment table. "That's where I feel at home," he yelled over an AC/DC song. He began to walk through the crowd of students and added, "Look, Cisco and Brad beat me to the munchies."

Feeling more conspicuous than ever, and a bit shy

away from the basketball court, Brian followed Reggie around the large group of dancing students to where the obviously bored teacher-chaperones were standing. As a few students waved at both Reggie and him, including Lori Harper, Brian saw several of the players with their girl friends. He didn't see Clarence, LaMont, or Alvin, who lived too far away to make the trip just for a dance.

Brian and Reggie stopped near Coach Ford, who was talking with several other teachers. "Glad to see you both decided to come tonight," said the coach. "Get out on the floor and show me your moves, Reggie."

"Naw, man, I'm too tired from practice."

Coach Ford laughed. "That'll be the day."

After an hour of having refreshments and watching the basketball team's three popular ladies' men—Jeff Burgess, Nick Vanos, and Terry Hanson—dance with a variety of girls, Brian and Reggie and Tony found themselves standing with George Ross against a wall and looking at the clock. Brian saw Reggie look at Tony, who looked up at Brian, who nudged George.

"Let's play some ball," said Brian, smiling.

Reggie retrieved his basketball at the coat rack, and the four of them sneaked out of the cafeteria down to the gym. Reggie switched on half of the lights. Then they quickly removed their jackets and shoes and began a spirited two-on-two half-court game, with Reggie and George against Brian and Tony.

After ten minutes of action during which nobody kept score, Brian received a pass from Tony, faked up with the ball to get the usually steady George

Ross out of position, and drove down the right baseline to the basket for an easy dunk shot.

"Nice move," said Coach Ford from the doorway.

The four of them froze and tried to look innocent. Nobody spoke for several seconds, and then Coach Ford smiled. "I was getting a little tired of listening to AC/DC myself," he said, looking at his watch. "Why don't you three call it a night and head on home?"

Reggie smiled, then tossed a final shot into the hoop.

The coach walked over to Brian. "The way you went around Ross is how you should go to the basket all the time," he said. He smiled and patted Brian on the back. "Now do it against guys a little bigger than Ross."

And with the coach's praise still ringing in his ears, Brian put on his shoes, grabbed his jacket, and reluctantly left the gym with his friends.

# SEVEN

On Saturday morning, Brian could tell which players had stayed out too late the night before. The three guys who had been burning up the dance floor—Terry, Nick, and Jeff—dragged into practice only ten minutes before it was supposed to start, their eyes still half-closed. But as Coach Ford had promised earlier, the morning practice was going to be short and mostly a review of their offensive and defensive systems.

"We're ready to face Carroll on Tuesday night," Coach Ford announced. "You've all worked your butts off, and I'm looking forward to a great season."

Then to Brian's surprise, the B-team coach, Pat Young, arrived carrying a clipboard filled with papers. He waved at the team, then joined them. With his thick-lensed glasses, pale complexion, and five-seven height, Coach Young certainly didn't fit the generally accepted image of what a coach should look like.

"While you gentlemen were having a good time at the dance last night," said Coach Young, smiling at them and pushing his glasses farther up the bridge of his nose, "I was busy scouting Carroll's opening game. And though they looked pretty good in winning seventy-seven to fifty-five against a weak team, I think we should be able to overpower them under the boards. That is, if everybody works hard."

And while Brian and the other players listened intently, Coach Young told them everything they should know about their Tuesday night opponent, including a little about each of their players. Their star player was Louie Taggart, a short, sharpshooting guard who scored thirty-three points during the opening game.

Coach Ford pointed at Reggie. "He's all yours, Dupree," said the coach. "We'll be playing man-to-man defense the entire game, so you'll have lots of time to shut him down."

"Man, the dude's history already," said Reggie, slapping fives with Clarence and Cisco.

Coach Young pushed his glasses up on his nose and talked to Reggie. "Taggart doesn't like to go to his left to shoot his jump shots," he said. "So make him go that way by overplaying him slightly on his right side. When Stokley High did that a few times last night, Taggart made only two of nine shots."

Brian listened to all the detailed information and wondered how Coach Tubbs at Paintville ever won a game without a scouting report. Soon it was Brian's turn to learn about Carroll's starting center, Troy Harmon, a skinny kid who stood only six three.

"He'll play up on you, Davis," said Coach Young, "so you might have to dribble the ball and drive to the basket. You have a five-inch height advantage, so we should be able to get the ball to you under the hoop."

After Coach Young finished his scouting report, the varsity players shot free throws and ran through their offensive systems for an hour, before the coaches whistled them back to the midcourt jump-ball circle. They all placed their hands into the middle of a tight huddle, and after Coach Ford counted one, two, three, the players raised their hands and yelled "Beat Carroll!"

By the time Brian and the rest of the players and coaches left the gym at one o'clock, the Jefferson Patriots were mentally and physically ready to begin the season, and Brian could hardly wait.


On Sunday morning, despite the frigid weather, Reggie and Tony and Cisco stopped by Brian's aunt's house for a little shooting practice at the garage basketball court. They also wanted to discuss the Sunday sports section with its annual predictions for the Indianapolis high school basketball teams.

"Listen to this," said Reggie, reading from the newspaper. "'Brian Davis of Jefferson is one of the top big men in the state this year and is the reason we're picking the Patriots as the third best team in Indianapolis behind Westside and Lincoln North.' Now here comes the really good part. 'Jefferson is also led by returning seniors LaMont Jackson and Clarence Reed, as well as one of the city's top playmaking guards, junior Reggie Dupree.'"

Tony swished a jump shot through the basket fastened to the garage, then turned toward Reggie. "Yeah, but that sportswriter obviously doesn't know you the way we do. Maybe we oughtta tip him off."

Reggie ignored him. "They also say in here that Davis is one of the city's best centers along with Oscar Brown of Westside and that six-foot-ten dude Dexter Cole from Lincoln North. Man, I can't wait until we play both of 'em."

"Let's take care of Carroll first," Brian said.

Monday arrived with Brian and the other players starting to feel a little nervous about the Tuesday night game—and with the school alive with basketball fever. Yet for Brian, the school day seemed to last forever.

Most of the students, a lot of them dressed in red-white-and-blue outfits for the pep rally, wished Brian and his teammates good luck whenever they saw them in the hallways or the cafeteria. Even the teachers got swept up in the excitement—many of them shook pom-poms in the halls or wore white tricorne hats with "Go Patriots" sewn in red on the sides. The cheerleaders, including Lori Harper, walked around school in their red-white-and-blue uniforms, occasionally letting go with an organized cheer in the hallway.

School was dismissed an hour early and the students were told to report to the gymnasium. Brian and the other varsity basketball players stood nervously shuffling their feet in a group at midcourt while more than fifteen hundred people jammed into the gym. The cheerleaders began a series of yells to get the crowd in the mood.

As the entire student body finally got settled in the bleachers, Mr. Rhodes arrived at midcourt with a microphone stand and addressed the crowd.

"Okay," said the gray-haired principal, "Let's hear

it for the best basketball team in the city of Indianapolis!"

The crowd screamed.

"Who's going to win on Tuesday?" shouted Mr. Rhodes.

"Jefferson!" yelled the crowd.

"I can't hear you!" cried Mr. Rhodes, holding a hand to his ear.

"*Jefferson!*" shouted the students twice as loudly, and Brian thought the roof of the gym was about to come off.

Then as the noise died down, Mr. Rhodes said, "Now here is the best basketball coach in the city of Indianapolis, a former star player himself at Jefferson and at Purdue, Mr. Tom Ford!"

The crowd went wild again, and Coach Ford walked to the microphone. For the next few minutes, he talked about the team and its chances for the season, and then he said it was a great pleasure to introduce this year's team captain. The coach paused, and the players as well as the fans waited to see who it was going to be.

"This year's team captain is LaMont Jackson," he said at last, motioning for LaMont to join him at the mike.

After the loud cheers for the popular LaMont faded, Coach Ford introduced the rest of the varsity. Even though he was in front of his own fans, Brian felt his nervous stomach doing flip-flops. When his turn came, the crowd applauded and cheered wildly as he shuffled to his spot in a line facing the bleachers. Then the pep rally concluded with a few spirited instrumentals by the Jefferson High band and several fan participation cheers started by the cheerleaders.

As Brian and his teammates dressed in the locker room for a forty-five-minute shooting practice, Coach Ford stopped by and announced the starting five. He said it would be Dupree and Hanson at the guards, Jackson and Reed at the forwards, and Davis at center. The lineup was pretty much what Brian had expected. But before he left, the coach also mentioned he planned on using lots of substitutes during the season and that everybody should show up for the games ready to play.

"Man, he says that every year," said Reggie.

Alvin, Cisco, and George—the B-team graduates— put their arms around one another's shoulders. "Yeah, but this year he's got a good bench," said Cisco, smiling.

The other players tossed towels at the trio.


Tuesday afternoon the varsity and B-team players boarded a large touring bus for the three-hour trip to Carroll, Indiana. The six cheerleaders and their faculty advisor, Miss Kelley from the math department, also entered the bus and sat up front near the three coaches.

The trip was boring for Brian, except when Coach Williams playfully asked Reggie and some of the other players to remove their rap-music tapes from their jam boxes and play some old Motown tunes. Other than that, he and his teammates were left alone to get psyched for the upcoming game.

Brian and the others were shocked when they stepped from the bus and entered the tiny Carroll High gymnasium. It reminded Brian of some of the small country gyms he played in with the Paintville 'Huskers. Its seating capacity was supposed to be two thousand, but the building was so cramped that the first row of the bleachers on both sides of the court was almost on the sidelines. And the stage at one end of the court, where the Carroll school band was preparing its instruments, was no more than twenty feet from the basket support.

"That's why they call places like this band boxes," said Coach Williams, shaking his head.

While Coach Young's B team dressed and then began its warm-ups in the already full gym, Coach Ford told the varsity that the town of Carroll was a small factory town and that high school basketball games were the main form of community recreation. "And," he added, "these Carroll fans can be very loud and hostile sometimes. They have no respect for any visiting teams, so just ignore them and concentrate on the game."

Butterflies began to flutter in Brian's stomach.

During the final quarter of the B-team game, which Carroll was winning by twenty points, Brian and the other varsity players changed into their blue road uniforms and listened to some final pregame instructions from Coaches Ford and Williams. Then, after the dejected B-team players filed into the locker room, the Jefferson varsity, led by its captain, ran onto the floor and was greeted by a loud chorus of boos from the Carroll fans.

The Carroll varsity trotted onto the floor in their fancy purple-and-gold warm-ups, and amidst an ear-shattering mixture of cheers and loud music from the band, the two teams warmed up for twenty minutes or so. As they finished shooting around and the clock ticked off the final seconds before game time, Tony nudged Brian and pointed at the crowded bleachers near the Jefferson team bench.

"Your mom and your aunt," shouted Tony over the noise. "My folks are coming up with Cisco's dad."

Brian looked, and his mom and aunt Margaret waved at him and smiled from where they were sandwiched among several dozen other Jefferson fans. And as the horn sounded calling both teams to the sidelines, Brian ignored some jeers yelled in his direction by the Carroll fans and kept repeating to himself, *Be yourself, be yourself.*

# EIGHT

The game opened with Brian easily winning the tap over six-three Carroll center Troy Harmon. But then the Patriots showed their first-game jitters by throwing away several passes in the first minute of play, much to the delight of the rowdy Carroll fans. Luckily for Jefferson, the Carroll Greyhounds also seemed nervous and didn't take advantage of the mistakes, missing three easy shots.

"Come on, let's go!" shouted Terry Hanson as he ran downcourt to play defense. "We can beat these guys!"

Moments later Louie Taggart, the high-scoring Carroll guard, dribbled through the foul lane and toward his basket. Reggie, using his super-quick hands, batted the ball away and began to race downcourt toward the Jefferson basket. One of the officials blew his whistle and called Reggie for reaching in and slapping Taggart's arm.

"Say what?" Reggie said, his face a mask of surprise.

Coach Ford jumped off the Jefferson bench and raised his arms, and Brian heard him yell, "What kind of call was that? He didn't even come close to touching the guy."

The official nearest to where Brian was standing, a big guy with a red face, trotted over to Coach Ford and said over the loud noise, "Coach, sit down or we'll have to call a technical foul. You just let us call the game the way we see it."

Reggie stepped over to Brian. "Man, welcome to Carroll," he said. "We won't get too many calls tonight."

Tony nodded and said, "Yeah, we just got a large helping of home cooking, served by that big ref."

Brian saw Clarence adjusting his goggles. "Well, I guess we'll just have to kick some butts tonight. None of these country boys is gonna get a rebound."

"Just watch your fouls, guys," said LaMont. "They're going to call 'em tight."

The game resumed and Carroll made three shots in a row from long distance. Two of them were by Taggart, who caught Reggie sleeping on defense while he dribbled to his right. Then Jefferson finally got on the scoreboard. Reggie dribbled to the left side of the court, then quickly bounced the ball in front of him and used the crossover move to head toward the right where Brian was set up in the corner, his hand raised. Reggie threw a bullet pass to Brian. In one smooth motion he caught it and lofted one of his high-arching jumpers toward the basket, where it swished through.

Soon the bigger and more experienced Jefferson players began to shake off their early game nervousness. LaMont unleashed some of his quick play-ground fakes and feints and lost his bewildered defender, then drove to the basket for a slam dunk. Clarence, using his muscles to get the inside re-bounding position, grabbed a missed shot by Brian and stuffed it back into the basket. And later in the first quarter, Brian found himself suddenly open fifteen feet from the hoop. He caught a neat bounce pass from Terry and swished a jumper.

The first quarter ended with Jefferson leading 17–14, but in the final ten seconds, the big official with the red face had whistled Reggie for his second foul against Taggart. Brian ended the quarter with a team-leading eight points, sinking four of six shots from the outside, but had grabbed only one rebound.

Brian and his teammates huddled in front of the bench and toweled off. Coach Ford yelled something to the big red-faced official, who ignored him, then joined the Jefferson players.

"Forget about the officials," said Coach Ford, screaming to be heard over the loud music of the Carroll High band. "It's hard to get a call to go your way in this gym, so just play as if we're ten points down and really hustle."

"Man, I didn't even touch that guy," said Reggie.

"I know," said the coach, "but just forget it. Right now, we have to concentrate on taking advantage of their defensive mistakes." Coach Ford looked at Brian. "Vanos is in for you now, but when you go back after your breather, you oughtta take the drive to the basket that their little center is giving you."

As the band finished a loud number, the teams walked onto the court to begin the second quarter.

Besides having Nick in for Brian, Coach Ford also substituted Alvin for Reggie at one guard position and George Ross for Clarence at one forward spot. The Carroll lineup remained the same. Brian figured their starters would be tired in the second half.

The second quarter began with Louie Taggart taking advantage of Alvin Woolridge's inexperience. The short Carroll guard faked a drive to the middle, causing Alvin to overreact in his eagerness to guard him and almost fall backward. Then Taggart jumped straight up and swished a twenty-foot jumper for three points, tying the game at 17.

Terry dribbled the ball upcourt for Jefferson, but in a sudden change of defense, the Carroll guards double-teamed him and stole the ball. Taggart raced for the Carroll basket and received a perfect pass for a lay-up. Sitting on the bench, Brian looked up at the scoreboard as the Carroll fans exploded with a loud roar. It read Carroll 19, Jefferson 17.

The very next trip down the court, Terry avoided the double-team by waiting until the last moment to toss a pass to Alvin. The sophomore guard, suddenly free for an instant but overreacting, dribbled into the foul lane for a lay-up and charged into Carroll's skinny center, Troy Harmon. Again the Carroll fans screamed their delight. Brian just buried his head in a towel, as did Reggie sitting next to him.

The next few minutes saw Taggart and his Carroll teammates take a ten-point lead, 30–20. Nick, playing center for Brian, moved as if his shoes were made of cement. Troy Harmon, Carroll's center, who had seemed intimidated by Brian's height, drove around Nick as if he were a statue and sank two easy lay-ups. George Ross sank a ten-foot jump shot, but then while running downcourt raising his fist in celebration he forgot to get back and play defense. The kid he was supposed to be guarding sneaked away and received a nice pass from Taggart for an easy lay-up.

Coach Ford called a time-out, and the fans went wild.

"Look, guys," said the coach, keeping his cool. "I understand this is the first game and we're playing in a small gym. But that's no reason to play stupid ball. We're not thinking out there. Carroll doesn't have anybody who can guard Jackson, yet he hasn't touched the ball for the last two minutes. And, Woolridge, I know this is your first varsity game, but you don't just drive wildly into a pack of players. You gotta think and look around, then make up your mind what to do." Coach Ford checked the scoreboard. "All right, they've taken a ten-point lead. Davis, Dupree, and Reed are back in. Now let's get the lead back."

Come on, guys," shouted Terry.

"Man, this stinks," added Reggie. "Let's get 'em."

Brian tossed his towel back toward the bench and walked onto the court determined to be more of a dominating player. For the final three minutes of the quarter, LaMont took charge of the Jefferson offense. He used some more playground moves to shake free for a lay-up and got fouled in the process. Then the Jefferson captain received a pass in the right corner, faked his man out of position, drove toward the hoop . . . and passed off to Brian for an easy dunk.

"Way to go, baby," said LaMont to Brian as they ran downcourt to play defense.

With one minute to play in the first half, and with Carroll leading 31–25, Reggie suddenly began guarding Taggart from the moment the little guard received the inbounds pass downcourt. With only ten seconds to move the basketball across the half-court line, Taggart was unable to dribble past Reggie's tight defense, and after about eight seconds it seemed like Reggie was going to force him into a violation. But as Taggart approached the ten-second half-court line, he leaned into Reggie and bumped him away.

The red-faced official called a third foul on Reggie.

"No!" cried Reggie, shaking his head.

Brian heard Taggart say, "Yeah, you got me." Then he watched as Taggart gently tossed the basketball at Reggie's face and walked away, causing Reggie to grab the ball and throw a bullet pass at Taggart's back. The officials missed Taggart's pass to Reggie's face, but they both saw Reggie's toss at the little Carroll guard.

"Son," said the red-faced official, "you're outta the game." He pointed toward the locker room.

The Carroll fans were angry, and Brian saw several of them start to charge the floor in an attempt to get at poor Reggie. Coach Ford held Reggie back from going after Taggart, while at the same time he carried on a protest with the red-faced official. And by the time Reggie was escorted to the locker room by Coach Williams and order was restored on the court, Taggart calmly dropped in a free throw for the technical foul charged to Reggie for unsportsman-like conduct. But he made only one of the two free throws given him for Reggie's last foul. The score, with one minute remaining in the half, was Carroll 33 and Jefferson 25.

In the final sixty seconds, Brian received a bounce pass from Tony, who had replaced Reggie in the lineup, and immediately felt pressure from Carroll's

Troy Harmon on his back. Brian pivoted and turned to face the basket and took a step as though he were going to drive for a lay-up. Harmon quickly took two steps backward, and Brian leaped straight up and launched a ten-foot jumper into the basket.

Score: Carroll 33, Jefferson 27.

With only ten seconds remaining in the first half, Taggart faked to his left, getting Tony off balance, then dribbled to his right toward the basket. Brian, guarding Harmon on the far side of the court, gambled that high-scoring Taggart would try to score some points for himself and left Harmon unguarded. Taking two giant steps toward the basket, Brian arrived there at the same time as Taggart, who tried a twisting lay-up shot. Brian reached out and batted the basketball back down into Taggart's face. It smacked off him and out of bounds. The horn sounded, ending the half, and Brian just smiled at Taggart as the little guard checked his nose to see if it was bleeding.

In the locker room, Brian noticed that Reggie was still steamed at being tossed from the game. The shaven-headed guard was nearly crying at the way the officials missed Taggart's foul but caught his. And he saw that LaMont and Clarence and Terry, the seniors, were upset at being behind to the little kids from Carroll. Coach Ford told everybody to calm down, then consulted with Coach Williams for a moment before returning to the players.

"All right," said the coach, "things aren't as bad as they may seem. Sure we're behind, but they've been playing on adrenaline. Their fans are a great motivating force, and that's what made Taggart and the others look so good. By the way, Davis, great block on Taggart at the end."

"Yeah, man," said LaMont, slapping a high-five with Brian.

"Way to go, Davis," said Terry.

"That'll teach the little punk," Tony added.

Coach Ford continued. "They only played five guys most of the half, and they've got to be tired. So we're coming out in the second half with a full-court man-to-man press." The coach looked at Alvin. "You're in for Reggie, but use that speed of yours to advantage. You gotta play under control. And that goes for the rest of you, too. What happened to Reggie happens from time to time. Reggie got "homered" by the officials, who obviously were influenced by the crowd. But that's no reason for Reggie, or any of you, to lose your cool and strike back."

"But, Coach—" Reggie began.

Coach Ford held up a hand. "Let's use this incident as a lesson for later on. Don't let the other team force you into losing your cool. Right, Dupree?"

Brian saw Reggie sigh deeply, then nod slowly.

The second half began with LaMont, Terry, Clarence, and the others as pumped up as Brian had ever seen them. Brian easily won the opening jump and tapped the ball to LaMont, who immediately turned on his speed and raced to the basket for an uncontested dunk shot.

Score: Carroll 33, Jefferson 29.

"Get 'em!" yelled Coach Ford from the bench.

As soon as LaMont's shot had slammed through the net, Brian and his teammates moved to the players they were supposed to be guarding and pressed full court. By the time the Carroll players realized what was happening, they couldn't get the ball inbounds within five seconds as stated in the rules. The big red-faced official blew his whistle and gave the ball over to Jefferson.

The Carroll team seemed stunned and had trouble setting up a zone defense, which they had switched to in the second half. Clarence tossed the ball to Brian, who was immediately double-teamed by two shorter Carroll defenders. Looking over the heads of the smaller players, Brian spotted LaMont open under the hoop, and passed him the ball for an easy lay-up.

Score: Carroll 33, Jefferson 31.

On the following inbounds play, Taggart tried to pass the ball in to a teammate before Jefferson could set up its full-court press, but the teammate wasn't expecting the quick pass. LaMont stepped in, stole the ball, and slammed a dunk shot down through the basket. The Jefferson players on the bench leaped to their feet, LaMont raised a fist, and the Carroll coach jumped up and down as he called a sudden time-out for his team.

The score: tied at 33.

For the remainder of the third quarter, Jefferson dominated the smaller Carroll team. The Carroll coach was forced to use some young and inexperienced substitutes, and even put Louie Taggart on the bench for several minutes.

At the end of the quarter, the score was Jefferson 47, Carroll 41.

But with Nick in for Brian, and LaMont also getting a rest in favor of George Ross to start the fourth quarter, Carroll began a comeback. As Taggart and the other Carroll starters finally returned to the game one by one, Jefferson eventually lost its lead on a long three-point shot by Taggart, who dribbled to his right against the slower Tony.

Score: Jefferson 57, Carroll 57.

After Coach Ford called a time-out, his next to last, Brian, LaMont, and Alvin returned to the game, joining Clarence and Terry Hanson for the final four minutes. The Carroll fans were still yelling as loudly as before. Brian sensed everybody in the gym realized the game was going to be decided in the last minute or so.

For the next three and one-half minutes, Carroll and Jefferson traded hoops. LaMont was spectacular, driving to the hoop once for a basket. Then he hit a fifteen-foot jumper on the next trip down the floor when his defender played back daring him to shoot. Brian found that the Carroll coach had decided to double-team him whenever he received the ball. He felt frustrated because he couldn't shoot or drive, only pass. The one time he did try to drive around both defenders, with one minute to go in the game and the score tied at 63–63, he dribbled the ball off his foot and out of bounds.

"Come on, man," yelled LaMont to Brian as they began to play defense. "Take better care of the ball." He patted Brian on the back. "Now let's get the ball back. Play tough 'D.'"

Fortunately for Brian, Taggart tried to be a hero and charged into Alvin on Carroll's next try for a basket. Jefferson got possession of the ball with twenty-two seconds to play. As the Carroll fans booed the big red-faced official for calling charging on Taggart, Coach Ford called his last time-out.

As the Carroll band rocked the gym with a loud number and the Carroll crowd yelled, Brian and the other Jefferson players had to huddle very closely to the coach in order to catch what he was saying. But finally, he set up a last-second play: Clarence was to

pass the ball inbounds to Brian, because Brian
was the tallest player on the court; Brian would
then pass or hand off the ball to Terry, who, with
about five seconds to play, would look for either
LaMont or Brian under the basket for a quick jump
shot.

The band stopped playing, but the Carroll fans
kept hollering, and the noise inside the little gym
was deafening. Clarence had no problem inbounding
the ball to Brian over the outstretched hands of
Carroll's center, Troy Harmon. But with Carroll
using a full-court pressing defense, Brian spent
nearly four seconds just trying to pass the ball off to
Terry, who was being closely guarded. Terry finally
grabbed the ball from his hand before an official
could whistle Brian for holding it for five seconds
and began to set up their play. Only sixteen seconds
remained in the game.

Brian ran under the basket and tried to get free for
one of his high-arching jumpers, but Harmon was
grabbing and clutching at him and he couldn't shake
him. LaMont appeared to be open for a second, but
the Carroll defenders were playing great defense and
he was soon well-guarded again.

Brian looked at the clock: 0:10, 0:09, 0:08, 0:07.

He raised his hand asking for a pass from Terry,
while being careful not to lean against Harmon and
draw an offensive foul. Suddenly he was open under
the hoop for a split second. Terry saw him but was
out of position to make a pass, and grimaced at
missing an opportunity to score.

The seconds ticked away: 0:06, 0:05, 0:04.

Shoot the ball!" yelled Coach Ford from the
bench.

Brian looked up at the clock: 0:03, 0:02.

He saw Terry Hanson fake a pass to LaMont. The man guarding Terry fell backward a little, and Terry leaped into the air and began to shoot an eighteen-foot jump shot.

# NINE

Just after Terry shot, the game-ending horn sounded. As Brian stood frozen under the hoop with the other players, he watched as Terry's long jumper hit the front of the rim, bounced off the back of the rim, rolled around the entire hoop, and then dropped through the basket for the game-winning two points.

The Jefferson substitutes raced onto the floor.

Brian and the other players already on the court raised their hands in celebration.

And soon Terry Hanson, smiling from ear to ear, was engulfed by the Jefferson team. Cisco, Reggie, and big Jeff Burgess reached him first and piled on top of him, slapping high-fives and screaming with joy. Brian and the others followed, and the pile of players on the court resembled the mass of bodies during a goal-line stand in a football game.

As the team finally ran toward its locker room, Brian saw the Carroll coach walk right by Coach

Ford's extended hand and refuse to shake following the hard-fought Jefferson victory.

In the locker room, Coach Ford finally managed to get everyone's attention and smiled broadly. "The outcome was never in doubt," he said, playfully wiping some sweat from his brow.

Brian and the other players cheered.

"We still have lots of things to work on," continued the coach, "but a win is a win, even if it was ugly to watch."

The players laughed, and cheered again.

"You guys on the bench who came in for the starters," added Coach Ford, "need to work on keeping the other team in check while the starters get some rest. But we have plenty of time to work on that and everything else." He looked at Terry Hanson and gave him a high-five. "Nice shot," said the coach.

"All right, Terry!" Tony shouted. "You're Captain Clank no more, baby!"

"Man, he's Captain Clutch now," said Reggie.

On the long bus ride back home through the darkened Indiana countryside, Brian thought about his performance in the opening game and wasn't too pleased with himself. While he did manage to score fifteen points on six-for-eight shooting, as well as three for three from the free-throw line, he only grabbed four rebounds and blocked just two shots. He figured a six-eight center ought to be a little more dominating, especially when they faced teams that were bigger and better than the Carroll Greyhounds.

As the team's scorebook was passed around to the various varsity players and finally reached Brian, he noticed that LaMont led the Jefferson scorers with

twenty-eight points, followed by Brian and then
Clarence with ten. Terry scored four, two of them on
his game-winning shot, while Reggie had three
points, Alvin and George two apiece, and Nick a
single free throw. Louie Taggart of Carroll led all
scorers with forty points, eighteen of them on long
three-point shots from beyond the nineteen-foot-
nine-inch line.

At least Jefferson was 1 and 0 for the season.


At school the following day, the Jefferson varsity
was tired from having arrived back in Indianapolis at
one-thirty in the morning, but happy just the same.
All the players spent the day receiving congratula-
tions from students and teachers alike.

The practice session that afternoon was spent
going over the mistakes made in the Carroll game,
and on shooting drills and free throws. Later they
went over a scouting report one of the coach's
buddies had prepared on the Oakridge Panthers, a
city team and their opponents for the home opener
on Friday night.

That evening Brian fell asleep doing his homework.


The next day, Brian was called from his second
period study hall by a voice on the intercom and told
to report to Coach Ford's office in the gym. After
walking through the empty hallways and past a
freshman PE class, he reached the coach's small
office and saw him sitting behind his battered gray
metal desk. The office was cluttered with PE equip-

ment and gym padlocks, since the coach was also the head of the PE department.

"Come in, Brian, and sit down," said Coach Ford, indicating a pair of scarred wooden chairs in front of the desk. "I figured you wouldn't mind taking a break from study hall."

Brian lowered his long lean body into one of the uncomfortable hard-backed chairs. "At the beginning of each season, and again toward the end, I like to have brief talks with all of the varsity players. You know, sort of question-and-answer sessions to make sure everything is all right with basketball, school, home."

Brian nodded. "Reggie told me about the talks."

"Well, there's not much to these little chats," said Coach Ford. "I just want all my players to know that I really do care about them, and that if they ever need a friend to help 'em out, I'm right here. Just like the other night at the rec center."

Brian nodded, and then he spotted the two dozen or so trophies in a glass-enclosed case behind the coach. He saw several large basketball trophies with old nets draped over them.

"So," Coach Ford continued, "what do you hear from your dad these days? Is everything all right?"

Even though he knew the coach was aware of his family problem, the question caught Brian off guard. "Yeah, I guess everything's fine. He's still living in Oklahoma with my uncle, and from what I hear his drinking problem is under control." Brian looked down at his feet and suddenly felt self-conscious. "At least that's what he tells me in his letters."

Coach Ford nodded and picked up a sheet of paper, then said, "Well, I know all about your schoolwork." He ran his finger down a list of names. "All Bs and Cs. Not bad."

Then the coach smiled. "Okay, now what about your basketball? What do you think about your play so far?"

Brian shrugged his slender shoulders. "I figure I've got lots of things to work on, but I've made some progress, too." He smiled. "And I'm getting used to the rougher city ball. Heck, I've got the bruises to prove it."

Coach Ford chuckled. "Now all you got to do is learn how to take advantage of situations during a game. You know, like when the opposing center plays back and challenges you to shoot, then you gotta shoot the ball. Although once the word gets around about your shooting ability, not many teams are going to let you fire the ball up so much."

Brian nodded. "Which means I gotta drive to the basket more when they start playing up close to me."

"Right," said the coach. "And you have to practice going to the basket. Learn how to get that all-important first quick step to the basket." Brian watched as Coach Ford put a cassette tape into a nearby VCR unit and switched on the TV next to it. "And you don't necessarily have to be naturally quick to get that first step advantage. Most of it comes by knowing when and how to fake a man out of position."

The VCR and TV came to life, and Brian saw Larry Bird of the Boston Celtics making some fancy one-on-one moves under the basket during a regular NBA game. Then Coach Ford pushed a button, and Brian saw some more of Bird's moves but in slow motion this time. And every time, Bird just used a little fake to get his defender off balance and out of position.

"See, Bird is really a slow guy who knows when and how to fake his defender out of his jock strap. And his great outside shot makes his drives more effective. There's really not that much to it except lots of practice and concentration."

"Yeah, but he's Larry Bird," said Brian, feeling like a lousy player by comparison. "I can't make moves like his."

"Sure you can. You're better than you think."

Brian heard lots of shrill screams as well as the patter of several dozen pairs of sneakers, and turned to watch the PE class head downstairs to the locker room.

Coach Ford stood and grabbed a basketball. "Come on," he said, smiling at Brian, "let's play a little one-on-one before your next class. It'll give you a chance to practice some moves to the basket."

Brian looked at his coach, a lean and fit former all-American at Purdue, and smiled sheepishly. "Me, against you?" he said.

And before he knew what he was doing, Brian had changed into his basketball shoes and was standing at the top of the key guarding Coach Tom Ford. The coach began to dribble, took a quick step to his right, getting Brian a little off balance, then made a quick crossover dribble and raced to his left. Brian recovered, but was a bit too late to make a defensive play and watched as the coach laid the ball in just before he could bat it away.

"Keep your balance," said Coach Ford. "You big guys have to bend over and get into a good defensive crouch."

Then it was Brian's turn to go on offense, and

before he could even dribble the ball several feet toward the basket, the coach used his hands to slap it away and begin his own offensive moves again. Coach Ford then scored four straight baskets and stopped Brian three more times before he could even get off one of his deadly jump shots, which missed this time. Brian felt his frustration building, and he wondered whether he would ever have enough offensive moves to beat somebody with even half the experience of Coach Ford.

The bell sounded, ending the period, and the freshman PE class filed slowly by, most of them stopping to watch the one-on-one matchup. "Keep playing," said the coach. "You can do it, just make your moves."

With sweat dripping down his face, Brian took the ball to the top of the key and began to dribble, turning his back on the smaller coach and backing him in toward the area in front of the basket. Coach Ford appeared to realize this and tried to push and shove Brian out of the foul lane. But once Brian felt the contact of the coach's forearm on his back, he spun quickly and took a giant step toward the basket. Coach Ford nearly fell over, and Brian leaped as high as he could and slammed the ball down through the hoop.

The freshman PE students, watching nearby, cheered.

Coach Ford smiled and gave Brian a high-five. "Just like Larry Bird," he said.

And as Brian changed shoes, he realized his coach had taught him an important lesson, and he could barely wait to use his new offensive moves in the first home game of the season on Friday night.

# TEN

While the girls' varsity teams from Jefferson and Oakridge played the preliminary game before a capacity crowd at the Jefferson High gym, Brian and his teammates sat in front of their lockers. Wearing their home white uniforms, they listened to the final pregame remarks from Coaches Ford and Williams.

Oakridge was a large public school only a dozen blocks away from Jefferson, and the two were always great rivals. So according to Coach Ford, although the game was Jefferson's home opener, many of the fans in the gym would be Oakridge supporters. The coach also reviewed the Oakridge team.

"Oakridge is not like Carroll," Coach Ford said. "They're a big, slow ball club that depends on two guys for most of their points. Bingo Stewart is a dead-on shooting forward who scored twenty points in their first game on Tuesday."

Coach Williams tapped Clarence on the shoulder.

"He's your man, Reed," he said. "Play up on him and take away his outside shot. Dare him to drive to the basket, then take that away, too, by playing good quick defense with your feet."

Clarence, pulling down his goggles from where they'd been resting on top of his head, nodded. "That dude won't score many points tonight," he said.

"Their other top scorer is a real monster," said Coach Ford, smiling. "His name is Hugh McCoy, and he stands six feet six and weighs two hundred and fifty pounds."

"Man, a regular animal," said Reggie, shaking his head.

"He's nothing," said football star Jeff Burgess in a soft voice. "Davis can handle him. McCoy was an all-city football lineman, but he's real slow."

Coach Ford nodded, and Brian saw him look toward him. "Drive on him, Davis, if he comes out after you."

"The only other real scoring threat is a little sophomore guard named Ollie Wright," added Coach Ford.

Brian saw Reggie nod his head. "I know that dude," he said. "Ollie's from my part of town. He's real skinny, but he can jump. And he likes to shoot from the corners."

"Then he's yours," said Coach Ford, "just to keep it in the neighborhood. But take it easy tonight. If he tosses the ball at you or takes a swing at your head, just back off and let the officials take over. Let's all learn from our mistakes up at Carroll."

The girls' game ended with Jefferson routing Oakridge 47–23. And once the court was cleared, Brian and his teammates ran onto the floor while the Jefferson High band played a rousing fight song. Lori

Harper and the other cheerleaders, waving pom-poms and even doing some cartwheels, ran along-side the varsity players. As Brian trotted to one of the two lines for lay-up shooting, he spotted his mom and his aunt seated beside Mr. Rhodes near the Jefferson bench.

Soon the Oakridge players ran onto the court amidst almost as much fanfare as the Jefferson team had received. Brian immediately spotted Hugh Mc-Coy, the big white center, who looked like a giant fire hydrant in his bright red warm-up suit.

After twenty minutes of lay-ups and shooting, the two captains, LaMont for Jefferson and Hugh McCoy for Oakridge, met at midcourt with the officials to shake hands and to make sure they all knew who the captains were in case of problems during the game. Then a buzzer sounded, and the teams trotted to their respective benches. A three-student fife-and-drum corps, led by the Jefferson High mascot decked out in tricorne hat and Colonial army uni-form and holding an American flag, then marched onto the court playing "Yankee Doodle."

As everyone in the gym rose, the band took over and played the national anthem, which was followed by a loud cheer as the mascot and the other students left the floor. Following the introduction of the starting lineups, Brian and the same lineup that started at Carroll walked onto the court. They were followed by the Oakridge starting five, dressed in their bright red road uniforms.

The official standing in the midcourt circle checked with the official scorer, then tossed the ball up between Brian and McCoy to open the game. Brian won the jump, and tapped the ball to LaMont. But Oakridge's Bingo Stewart, anticipating the play, reached in and batted the ball to Ollie Wright, their skinny sophomore guard.

"I got him," yelled Reggie, getting into a defensive crouch and immediately bothering Wright.

Brian ran downcourt alongside the massive Hugh McCoy, who began elbowing him immediately, and watched as Reggie stuck real close to the skinny Ollie Wright. Obviously neighborhood pride was at stake between the two, and Brian knew Reggie wasn't going to let the sophomore Oakridge guard get the best of him.

Before Wright could even dribble a dozen times, Reggie reached in and neatly stole the ball from him. LaMont and Brian both spotted the steal and turned to run a three-player fast break with Reggie. The other Oakridge players, setting up their offense, were caught unaware. Soon Reggie was dribbling by himself, with Brian and LaMont approaching on the wings, and slam-dunked the ball into the basket.

The Jefferson fans exploded with a loud roar.

"Way to go," LaMont said to Reggie.

The very next trip down the floor, Ollie Wright dribbled a few times, with Reggie hounding him, then passed off to the slower and shorter senior guard beside him. As Reggie ran upcourt with the frustrated Wright alongside, Brian noticed a satisfied smile on Reggie's lean black face.

The Oakridge guard passed the ball to Bingo Stewart, who was being closely guarded by Clarence. Stewart tried a move to his right, but the forward was cut off at the baseline by Clarence and passed the ball back to the senior guard. But the guard, apparently used to having Stewart shoot all the time, wasn't prepared for a return pass. Terry

Hanson stepped between the two Oakridge players and intercepted the pass.

Because so many Oakridge players were back on defense, Terry couldn't fast break. So he slowed up, shouted out the number for a play involving Brian, and then dribbled upcourt to start the offense.

Brian heard the play and ran to the baseline with McCoy staying with him step for step. Brian faked back and forth along the baseline several times, causing the overweight McCoy to bob to and fro like a puppet on a string, then cut toward the free throw line. Clarence had just set a pick there, and before Brian could receive a pass, McCoy smashed into Clarence like a football linebacker breaking through the line. Clarence bounced off McCoy and went sprawling to the floor.

One of the officials blew his whistle and charged McCoy with a foul. Jefferson was awarded the ball out-of-bounds, but first Brian and LaMont helped the shaken Clarence to his feet.

"Man," said Clarence, readjusting his goggles, which had been knocked at an angle in the crash, "that was like getting hit by a truck."

As Clarence passed the ball in to Terry to resume play, Brian began to make some offensive fakes. He noticed McCoy was standing five feet away with his hands on his hips. Brian raised his right hand and called for the ball.

Terry spotted Brian's raised hand and fired a bullet pass to him about fifteen feet from the hoop. Brian caught the ball, leaped into the air, and swished a jump shot over the suddenly startled McCoy.

LaMont played tough defense downcourt, forcing his man to take a bad shot at the Oakridge basket.

Brian pulled down the rebound and snapped a quick outlet pass to Reggie near midcourt to start a fast break. But the Oakridge players were already back on defense, so Reggie slowed down and set up Coach Ford's passing offense—and soon found Brian alone again on the baseline, McCoy standing away from him.

Brian caught Reggie's perfect chest pass, took aim at the hoop, and calmly lofted another fifteen-footer into the basket. As Brian began to run downcourt to play defense, he spotted Hugh McCoy shaking his head and spreading his arms in a "what can I do?" gesture.

For the remainder of the first quarter, the Jefferson Patriots dominated the game. Brian hit two more long jumpers, as McCoy refused to guard him away from the basket. LaMont and Clarence controlled the rebounds on both ends of the court, and Terry Hanson, apparently glad to have shed the nickname Captain Clank, hit two long three-point shots. When the quarter finished, the score was Jefferson 22, Oakridge 12.

The Jefferson fans cheered and the pep band played a spirited number.

Brian started the second quarter resting on the bench along with Clarence, LaMont, and Terry. Nick began the quarter at center, while Coach Ford inserted Brad Cunningham, seeing his first action of the season, at one forward and George Ross at the other. Reggie remained as the only member of the starting five still on the court, and was joined at guard by Tony Zarella. The Oakridge coach also made several changes, including giving Hugh McCoy a rest.

"Remember, you guys," Coach Ford called out as

the Jefferson players walked onto the court, "try to keep the game under control while the starters are sitting down. You can do it."

But as Brian and the four other starters watched glumly from the bench, the Jefferson High subs once again failed to hold the lead. Within two minutes, Nick fumbled away three passes. And when McCoy returned to the game, he let the big Oakridge center push him around under the hoop for easy offensive position—and four baskets, as well as three quick fouls on Nick. When Coach Ford inserted Alvin Woolridge for Reggie, the quick sophomore guard played out of control for the second straight ball game. He threw two wild passes, one of which nearly struck a Jefferson cheerleader in the head, and traveled on two other occasions. And when Jeff Burgess entered the game, his first that season, he looked slower than McCoy and couldn't stop the Oakridge center any better than Nick Vanos had.

Coach Ford called a time-out. Brian looked up at the scoreboard to see that the score was Jefferson 33, Oakridge 30.

"We need some help from you substitutes," said Coach Ford, shaking his head. "We have to get some production from you guys or soon the other teams are gonna start using full-court presses. And they'll keep on pressing us because they know our bench won't hurt them once we give our starters a rest."

Brian and the entire starting unit returned to the game for the final two minutes of the first half. Immediately Reggie took charge again. He stole the ball from Wright, drove down the entire court, and slammed the ball down through the basket.

The Jefferson fans went wild again. The cheer, "Go, Patriots, go! Go, Patriots, go!" echoed through the large gym. Brian felt his adrenaline beginning to surge. He gave Reggie a high-five, then turned and watched as Ollie Wright passed the ball in to McCoy near the Oakridge basket. The big center turned but lost his balance as he tried to shoot a jumper. Brian leaped and blocked the weak shot almost before it left McCoy's hand. Then Brian caught the ball and passed it to Reggie, who was streaking downcourt.

Reggie faked and feinted past Wright and once again slammed the ball through the hoop, sending the Jefferson rooters into another frenzy of loud cheers. Finally the first half ended with the score Jefferson 37, Oakridge 32, and Brian and his teammates trotted to the locker room.

While the music from the Jefferson pep band filtered through the walls, Coach Ford kept his cool but told everybody he wasn't pleased with their performance so far.

"We should be burying these guys by twenty points," he said, pacing back and forth. "We've stopped their top scorers so far, and they've played poorly against our scorers. But their coach isn't stupid. He'll make changes, so we better be ready for a real tough second half."

And as Brian and the other starters began the third quarter, they quickly realized that the Oakridge team had indeed made some changes. First, Hugh McCoy was now guarding Brian closely, thus making it more difficult for him to shoot his long jumpers. On offense they began running more picks against the Jefferson man-to-man defense, allowing Bingo Stewart to get open for his first few jump shots of the game. Finally, they began using McCoy as one of the largest picks Brian had ever seen, and Ollie

Wright started cutting around him for several easy jump shots.

For Jefferson, Brian was completely stopped from getting off his deadly jumpers, and he felt helpless. Every time he received a pass from Reggie or Terry, Hugh McCoy or Bingo Stewart would be right in front of him waving their hands. And on the two occasions when Brian tried to drive around them, he dribbled the ball off his foot once and crashed into McCoy for an offensive charging foul on the second try.

The third quarter ended. Jefferson 49, Oakridge 48.

"Man," said Reggie, shaking his head and trudging to the Jefferson bench, "we should've stomped all over these bums in the first half when we had 'em down."

Brian toweled off and listened as Coach Ford tried to get their spirits up for the tough fourth quarter just ahead. But with his poor offensive drives and his inability to shoot the ball in the second half, Brian barely listened to the coach. Instead, he burned with anger and determination and looked forward to redeeming himself in the last quarter.

But the fourth quarter was the same as the third, and Oakridge seemed inspired by their ability to stop Brian and LaMont from scoring either by jump shots or drives to the basket. And midway through the final quarter, Bingo Stewart jumped into the air for a shot. LaMont, who had switched over to Stewart after Clarence had gotten caught in a pick set by McCoy, leaped with him and tried to block the shot. The ball swished through the basket, but when LaMont landed he stepped on top of Stewart's left foot, twisting his ankle.

As the lean Jefferson captain lay on the floor wincing with pain, Brian saw the dejected looks on the faces of Reggie, Clarence, and his other team-mates. He knew how much the team looked to LaMont for leadership and scoring, especially when they needed an important basket during a close game. Coach Williams helped LaMont limp off the court.

With four minutes left to play, Coach Ford sent Tony into the game to play guard and moved Reggie over to LaMont's forward position. "Man, I'm not letting these dudes beat us," said Reggie. "Let's put it to 'em."

The action began with Bingo Stewart and Ollie Wright scoring easily on drives to the basket and outside shots. Tony let Wright drive past him twice for easy lay-ups, and with only two minutes remaining, Brian wondered if Jefferson was about to let an apparent victory slip away from them. The score was Jefferson 62, Oakridge 60.

As the seconds ticked away, Brian couldn't score against the close guarding of both McCoy and Bingo Stewart, but he did make a nice pass under the basket to Reggie, who cut for a lay-up. With fifteen seconds left to play, the Patriots led 68–66.

The Jefferson fans roared, and Oakridge called time.

# ELEVEN

"All right," said Coach Ford in the time-out huddle, "we're going to switch to a two-one-two zone defense. They've only seen us play man-to-man, so maybe this'll shake 'em up a little and throw off their last-second shot."

Brian leaned forward and tried to listen to the coach over the deafening music of the Jefferson pep band, his mind focusing on the change of defenses and where he was supposed to play in the zone. His only mission: Stop Oakridge.

"I want Davis and Reed under the basket on the zone, with Dupree in the foul lane. Hanson and Zarella, play out front and put pressure on the man with the ball."

The buzzer sounded, ending the time-out period.

"Okay, guys," said Coach Ford, standing. "We've let Oakridge back into this game, but now let's keep 'em from scoring and we've got it!"

"Man, let's stop 'em!" shouted Reggie.

LaMont limped over to Brian. "Don't give 'em a lay-up," he said, patting Brian on the back.

As Brian walked onto the court with his teammates and the Oakridge players, he looked into Hugh McCoy's eyes hoping to see a hint of what the Oakridge plan was. But all he noticed was the weariness of the big football player, whose red uniform was soaked with perspiration.

All the fans in the gym were standing. Brian could almost feel the tension in the air. He lined up next to McCoy under the Oakridge basket and watched as Bingo Stewart tossed the ball in to their stocky senior guard, who then stopped and dribbled in place for a few seconds. Brian saw the confusion on the puzzled kid's face as he suddenly noticed that the Jefferson players were using a zone defense.

Brian heard the Oakridge coach yell, "Move the ball!"

Then Brian stole a glimpse at the clock and watched the seconds tick away: 0:11, 0:10, 0:09.

The senior guard dribbled around the top of the key while Tony and Terry tried to bother him a little. But the two Jefferson guards stayed in their tightly packed zone defense and guarded against any easy lay-ups down the middle.

Brian watched McCoy and thought that, although the big center hadn't attempted another shot since having his jumper slapped away by Brian, he could be the player the Oakridge team would go to for the last shot.

The clock kept ticking: 0:06, 0:05, 0:04.

Then suddenly out of the corner of his eye, Brian saw Ollie Wright dash past him on the baseline and around Hugh McCoy's massive body. Before Brian could fight his way past McCoy, Wright received a

pass from the senior guard. The sophomore leaped
high into the air and released a soft fifteen-foot
jump shot. As the clock reached 0:01, the ball
swished through the net. Time ran out, and the
buzzer sounded ending the game with the score tied,
68–68.

The Oakridge players raised their hands and
screamed with joy, then mobbed Ollie Wright. Their
fans went crazy in the bleachers while the Jefferson
team just looked at the scoreboard as if they
couldn't believe their eyes.

Back at the bench, Brian and his teammates
toweled off, and the coach prepared them for their
first overtime game of the season. "Look, those
Oakridge kids are really tired," he said, nodding in
the direction of the visitors' bench. "They may be
happy now, but I guarantee you that big McCoy isn't
looking forward to three more minutes against you
guys."

Coach Williams nodded. "You oughtta be able to
run against them," he added in his deep baritone
voice. "And you should drive to the basket quick
'cause those dudes are dragging their butts and
won't be able to stay with you."

The buzzer sounded, and as the fans for both sides
began to shout encouragement to their heroes, Brian
led Reggie, Terry, Clarence, and Tony onto the floor
for what they all hoped would be the final three
minutes of the game.

Brian won the jump to start the overtime and
tapped the ball to Reggie. He noticed how exhausted
McCoy seemed when he barely jumped. Brian immediately turned and raced ahead of McCoy downcourt
toward the Jefferson basket, his right hand outstretched asking for the ball.

Reggie spotted him and passed the ball to Brian. But Hugh McCoy caught up and was lumbering toward him.

Reggie's pass arrived in Brian's hands only a second before McCoy reached the spot where Brian was standing—about seventeen feet from the basket. Brian caught the pass and took one step forward. McCoy tried to react with a quick step backward but lost his balance and almost fell to his knees. Brian took advantage of McCoy's awkward position and lofted a long jumper that swished through the net.

Before the fans could even finish cheering for Brian, Clarence blocked a lay-up attempt by McCoy ten seconds later down at the Oakridge end. Tony grabbed the loose ball and passed downcourt to Brian, who stopped fifteen feet from the Jefferson basket and swished another jumper over Bingo Stewart's outstretched hand.

The remainder of the overtime belonged to the Jefferson Patriots, as Clarence blocked another shot and Brian hit his third jump shot in a row. Ollie Wright swished a three-point shot at the final buzzer, but the game ended with a score of Jefferson 74, Oakridge 71.

"Well, guys, your physical conditioning paid off tonight," Coach Ford said as the team got undressed. "But there were lots of mistakes out there tonight. Zarella, you got to stick to your man. Vanos and Ross, we need more hustle, less hesitation. And, Dupree, you . . ."

After the coach finished and left to talk with Coach Williams, Cisco Vega said, "Hey, you'd think we lost the game the way coach was carrying on about our mistakes."

Brian looked up from unlacing his sneakers and watched as LaMont, an ice pack taped to his mildly sprained ankle, hobbled past. "Coach is right," said LaMont, glancing at Cisco. "We didn't play too cool tonight. We need to kick some butt over at Terre Haute next weekend to make these other teams respect us."

As the other players showered and dressed, Brian felt happy about the victory but still wished he could have played more like Coach Ford wanted him to play: drive to the basket for easy lay-ups like Larry Bird. Then Brian looked at the varsity scorebook. He noticed he had held Hugh McCoy to only four points and had scored twenty-two points himself with his long jumpers. Suddenly he felt a little better, even more so when he realized Jefferson was 2 and 0 for the season.

Brian returned to school on Monday to find he was a star in the eyes of both Mr. Bandiwell and Lori Harper. In fact, the victory over Oakridge turned all of the Jefferson varsity players into instant celebrities.

"Man, nothing beats winning," said Reggie at Monday's practice.

"Think we'll go unbeaten this year, Reg?" asked Cisco.

Reggie shrugged. "We'll know more after this tournament in Terre Haute," he said. "You're gonna see some bad dudes over there. If we can handle them, who knows?"

The team and coaches were looking forward to

traveling to the western Indiana city of Terre Haute
for a two-game weekend tournament. The famous
early season tournament was hosted by a big high
school, Terre Haute Roosevelt, and was called the
"Big Four" Tournament. Three top Indiana basketball schools were invited by Roosevelt to the tournament every year, and the trip meant an over-
night stay in a Holiday Inn for Brian and his teammates.

But by Wednesday, Brian noticed Reggie and
several of the other players were acting sort of
cocky because of the team's win-loss record of 2 and
0. He even noticed that he, too, wasn't working as
hard as he had been before the two victories. Coach
Ford must have noticed also, because at practice he
yelled and screamed more than he had all season,
and made the team run an extra few dozen fast
breaks as well as some wind sprints.

"We haven't faced any good teams yet," shouted
Coach Ford as Brian and his teammates ran their
tenth set of wind sprints on Thursday. " You're not
going to beat everybody just by showing up. Especially after barely winning our first two games in the
last seconds."

But Friday finally arrived, and the varsity was
dismissed from school at noon to make the long bus
trip across the state to Terre Haute. Besides the
twelve varsity players, the coaches, and the cheerleaders, Mr. Bandiwell and another teacher, Mr.
Paxson, came along as chaperones. And Miss Kelley
accompanied the cheerleaders, as usual.

Following a two-hour ride past dried cornfields
and rounded haystacks, the team arrived in the large
drab city of Terre Haute at about two-thirty. Then

they checked into a Holiday Inn a short drive from the Roosevelt gym.

Brian and Tony were paired as roommates, and as soon as they and all the other players changed into practice uniforms, the team climbed back into the bus and rode several miles to the Terre Haute Roosevelt gym for a one-hour practice session. The practice was really to get acquainted with Roosevelt's new nine-thousand-seat gym, which was actually an arena. Each of the three visiting teams was allowed an hour on the court that afternoon.

At four o'clock Brian and his teammates ate a steak dinner in a private dining room at the Holiday Inn, then dressed in their white uniforms and blue warm-ups. They were scheduled to play the first game of that evening's doubleheader at seven-thirty against the number-two-rated high school team in Indiana, the Wolfpack of Gary Tech. In the second game, the host school, Terre Haute Roosevelt, was scheduled to face the tough Clayville Zeniths from southern Indiana. A capacity crowd was expected for both games.

In the spacious new locker room about forty minutes before the game, Brian noticed that except for LaMont, who was always prepared, most of his teammates seemed less focused on the game than they had been prior to the first two games of the season.

Cisco was reading a copy of the scorecards being handed out to the fans when he said, "Hey, look, the Clayville team is called Zeniths." He laughed and added, "I wonder why they named their team after television sets."

The players laughed, until finally Coach Ford held up his hand and began his pregame talk.

"We've been over the Gary Tech scouting report," he said, "so I'm not going to mention their individual players much. They're a well-balanced team with lots of good players, but the best of the lot may be their six-five forward, Larry White. They're the fastest, most experienced team we'll face this season."

The coach paused, and Brian saw his teammates were beginning to get a little nervous.

"Also," added Coach Ford, "Gary Tech uses half a dozen different full-court presses during a game. Man-to-man or zone press, it doesn't matter to them. They'll just keep after you and try to force passing and ball-handling mistakes."

LaMont called a huddle, and the team locked hands, then yelled, "Beat Gary!" But when they trotted from the locker room and into the circular arena that was already jammed with nearly nine thousand excited fans, they spotted the Gary Tech players, dressed in black and gold, putting on a dunking exhibition for the crowd at the far end of the court.

Brian and the other Jefferson players paused in their lay-up shooting for a moment and watched the Wolfpack. All of them were black except for one big white guy, and every one of them dunked the ball during their warm-up drill—even their five-foot-seven-inch guard, who easily slam-dunked the ball and earned a standing ovation from the fans.

"Man, that's nothing," said Clarence, taking a pass as the Jefferson players resumed their lay-up drill. Then he ran up to the basket, soared into the air, and slammed the ball down into the hoop—but the ball struck the back of the rim and bounced twenty feet into the air.

The crowd jeered, and Clarence just shook his head.

Tony leaned toward Brian. "Maybe it's not going to be our night," he said, staring over at the Gary players.

# TWELVE

Brian felt a queasy, anxious sensation in his stomach as he lined up for the jump ball to open the game. His feelings of dread were reinforced immediately when Luther Spikes, Gary's six-foot-four-inch center easily out-jumped him and tapped the ball to Tech's five-foot-seven guard, Laverne Royce. The tiny guard flipped a perfect lead pass downcourt to their star forward Larry White, who brought the ball behind his head for a moment as he leaped, then slam-dunked it down through the basket.

The nine thousand fans cheered in appreciation of the tomahawk dunk, and as Brian tried to set up against the Gary full-court press, he heard cries of "Awesome!" from the fans.

Laverne Royce ran over to guard Reggie, who was waiting for Clarence to inbound the ball following the dunk shot.

Before Brian could think what to do next, the Gary center, Luther Spikes, was crouched in a defensive stance next to him, his big hands waving in Brian's face, distracting him. Brian looked quickly around the backcourt area and noticed all his teammates were being guarded so closely they couldn't even break toward Clarence to receive the inbound pass.

One of the officials blew his whistle and held up five fingers, indicating that Jefferson had failed to pass the ball inbounds within the five-second period as stated in the rules. Laverne Royce nodded vigorously as if saying it was a good call, then stepped out-of-bounds to await the ball from the officials.

Royce received the ball from one of the officials, then passed it quickly inbounds to the other guard, who returned it to Royce. Before Brian realized what was happening, Luther Spikes ran up behind LaMont and set a blind pick on him. Brian failed to stick with Larry White, LaMont's man, and White used the pick to cut to the basket, where he received a lob pass from Royce for another slam dunk.

The crowd nearly went berserk. Less than twenty seconds had run off the clock, and already Gary Tech was running the Jefferson Patriots into the floor.

Clarence finally managed to inbound the ball with a quick bounce pass to Reggie. At the same time, Brian turned to head upcourt, but he couldn't shake Spikes, who ran with him stride for stride.

As Brian reached the midcourt line, he turned and looked back just in time to watch Royce and his backcourt mate using a full-court zone press to trap Reggie against the sideline. Before Brian could run back to help, Reggie tossed a wild pass across the court toward Terry Hanson. A quick, six-foot-three Gary forward intercepted the pass and raced to their basket for a twisting lay-up shot over and around Clarence.

Coach Ford called a time-out.

With the crowd noise pounding in his ears, Brian slumped onto the bench beside his teammates. As he toweled off, he glanced quickly around the vast saucer-shaped arena and tried to calm down. He noticed the crowded grandstand swept up and away from the court so far that the faces of the fans in the last twenty rows were only a blur. The gym was really different from Carroll's tiny band box, and so was the game.

"Man," said Reggie, a look of disgust on his face.

"Those guys can fly," said Terry.

"They're just basketball players like you," said Coach Ford above the crowd noise. The coach knelt beside the bench. "All right, let's make the best of a bad situation. Against their press, don't panic—just set up the plays we ran in practice all week. Get back to the basics, that's all this game is. If we run our press plays right, then we should get a lay-up, or the other team will foul us."

The buzzer sounded, ending the time-out.

"Okay," said Coach Ford, standing now and looking up at the scoreboard. "Even with all the high-flying slam dunks, they're still only leading six to nothing. We can catch 'em."

"Let's go, guys!" LaMont yelled.

"Yeah, they're not *that* good," said Reggie as he walked out onto the court with Brian and Terry.

"Let's set up the press plays," said LaMont as they approached the far end of the court.

The official handed the ball to Clarence out-of-bounds, and he waited for the Jefferson players to get into position to combat the press.

"Break!" yelled Clarence, giving the signal to start the offense against a full-court press.

With Clarence's signal, Reggie and Terry broke in different directions in the backcourt. Downcourt, Brian faked a quick move to the sidelines as if he were about to receive a long pass. Seeing that Luther Spikes fell off balance for a moment, Brian then sprinted up to a spot just past midcourt and in the same halfcourt area where Clarence was trying to inbound the ball. LaMont was far downcourt.

Brian knew he was open for a split second, and he watched as Clarence hurled a forty-foot baseball pass in his direction. Just before Brian caught the speeding ball, Luther Spikes ran up behind him. Brian caught the ball with both hands and braced himself for some body contact with the speeding Gary center.

Unable to stop his momentum, Luther Spikes slammed into Brian in his attempt to steal Clarence's long inbound pass. The officials whistled him for a foul, and despite having the wind knocked out of him for a second, Brian had broken the full-court press at last.

Clarence tried to inbound the ball at half court. Brian and his teammates ran into the same pressure defense, only now it was a half-court trapping zone press. As Reed inbounded the ball to Reggie, Jefferson began working its offensive system against Gary Tech's pressing defense. Trying to get open by faking and running, Brian figured the Jefferson Patriots were in for a long, exhausting game.

For Brian, the first quarter was a blur of gold-shirted Gary Tech defenders leaping at him every time he received a pass, or double-teaming him and all his teammates each time a pass was made between two Jefferson players. Brian had never faced such a quick-moving, clinging defense, and other than one wide-open jump shot he swished when his defender slipped, he didn't even come close to having any scoring opportunities.

Only LaMont, with three quick drives around his leaping defender, was able to penetrate the Gary Tech defense during the first quarter. Slow-footed Terry Hanson seemed overwhelmed by the quick Tech guards, and Clarence was constantly being outjumped for rebounds at both ends of the floor. Reggie, who was just as fast as the Gary players, kept too busy helping out Brian and his other teammates to be a very effective force in the scoring.

At the end of one quarter, the score was Gary Tech 23, Jefferson 10.

The remainder of the first half didn't go much better for the Patriots. When Coach Ford substituted Alvin and Tony and Nick, the result was the same as before. Only a fine second quarter by Reggie, who scored ten points on drives to the basket around overanxious Gary subs, saved Jefferson from being completely routed by halftime.

Brian spent much of the second quarter on the bench, but when he finally returned, he managed to score two baskets on turn-around jump shots over the waving arms of Luther Spikes. Still, the game was a humbling experience for Brian and all his stunned teammates.

The score at the half: Gary Tech 52, Jefferson 30.

As Brian and the other players filed into the locker room with their heads down, Coach Ford just shook his head and said, "Well, at least things can't get any worse."

Brian thought the coach was surprisingly calm and unruffled by their horrible performance. He was used to Paintville coach Horace Tubbs's ranting and raving, with tobacco juice spraying all over the place, after his team had played poorly.

"Now you know what it's like to play a really good team," said the coach.

"Man, they gotta be the best team in the state," said Reggie, shaking his head and looking down at the floor.

Coach Ford nodded. "They're good," he said, "but I'll tell you guys something, they can't play any better than they did in the first half. They made very few mistakes on both offense and defense, and they were sky high for the game before they even set foot on the court." Brian saw Coach Ford shrug. "And to make things look better for them, we happened to play our worst game of the year at the same time."

Lifted a little by Coach Ford's encouraging words, Brian and the rest of the Jefferson Patriots returned for the second half and outplayed Gary Tech. Jefferson beat the Wolfpack's full-court presses, and ended up outscoring Gary in the half, 40–33. Brian managed to drive once around Luther Spikes, and he hit two more long jumpers against the Gary Tech subs later in the game.

The final score was Gary Tech 85, Jefferson 70. LaMont scored thirteen points in the second half, mostly on drives against the press, and led Jefferson in scoring for the game with nineteen points. For the game, Brian scored fourteen, with five rebounds, and Reggie added fifteen. Nobody else did much, except for Alvin Woolridge, who scored all four of his baskets in the second half against the Gary subs.

Back at the Holiday Inn that night, Coach Ford

told the players to forget about the loss but to learn from it. Everybody's spirits were better after Terre Haute Roosevelt blasted Clayville, Jefferson's opponent in the next day's consolation game, by the score of 93–65. Exhausted, the Patriots all went to sleep early.

"A consolation game is pretty lame for a tournament," said Cisco Vega at breakfast the next morning.

"Yeah, but you guys better be ready for Clayville just the same," said Coach Ford, sipping his coffee. "Clayville played as poorly as we did, so don't expect them to put two bad games back to back."

With Coach Ford's warning setting the tone for the day, Brian and the other players stayed in their motel rooms, except for a brief one-hour shoot-around at the arena, and got pumped-up for the Clayville game set for seven o'clock.

That evening in the locker room, Coach Ford said, "This Clayville ball club reminds me of Carroll. They're small and scrappy, and I think we can beat them, too."

Coach Williams added, "And they don't have a kid over six two, so we should have the advantage under the boards. But these dudes *can* shoot the ball, especially their top scorer, a forward named Tom Larsen."

As the game opened, with Jefferson using the same starting lineup, Brian quickly saw that they were too eager to win. Reggie fired two quick jumpers, LaMont one, and he shot what appeared to be a wide-open shot from the baseline—all of which missed. After Clayville took a 12–2 lead in the first four minutes, Coach Ford called a time-out.

Brian, and the other players, were shocked when Coach Ford shouted at them in anger for the first time this season, his face turning red. "Don't let this bunch of little guys make you look bad! Get out there and start to play up to your potential, or I'll make some changes and put in guys who will."

The threat worked miracles for the Jefferson varsity. Following the lead of LaMont, they played hard until they had scored the next eighteen points of the game, shutting out Clayville during that time by playing tight man-to-man defense. The Patriots grabbed the lead 20–12, and never looked back for the rest of the game.

For the remainder of the game, the Jefferson varsity played some smart ball. Since Brian was six inches taller than Clayville's tallest player, Reggie and LaMont and the others threw him plenty of sharp passes. He turned and shot into the basket all game long. And on defense, Jefferson held Clayville's top scorer to only ten points.

The final score was Jefferson 83, Clayville 79, but the game wasn't really that close. After Brian had scored a team-high thirty points, and with the team leading by fifteen with only three minutes remaining, Coach Ford took out the starters and used his bench: Brad, Alvin, George, Jeff, and Tony. But the bench played poorly and let Clayville close to within four points as the final buzzer sounded.

"Well, I guess third place is better than fourth," said Tony in the locker room after the game.

Coach Ford got the attention of the players. "Right, Zarella. It was a team effort," he said. He looked at Brian. "Great shooting tonight. You scored thirty points."

"Way to go, Davis," said LaMont.

The other players applauded and cheered.

"Now all you need to work on," continued Coach Ford, "is driving to the basket better against some of the good centers we'll be facing later in the season."

Brian pulled off his sweaty uniform and sighed. "I know, Coach, but how can I learn some good moves to the basket?"

Coach Williams smiled and patted Brian on the shoulder. "I think I know a way of helping you out," said the big coach, stroking his goatee thoughtfully. "We'll start as soon as we get back home." Coach Williams laughed deeply. "Davis, I'm going to introduce you to my secret weapon."

Both coaches laughed and left the locker room.

"Man, you looked good tonight," said Reggie, stepping over to Brian and giving him a high-five.

"Yeah, now we got us a center who can score," added LaMont, also slapping high-fives with Brian.

Brian's teammates gathered around and congratulated him. Even though he knew he had some moves to work on, he smiled and finally felt like a big-city center.

# Glossary of
# Basketball Terms

*Air ball*—A missed shot at the basket that sails through the air and fails to touch the rim, net, or backboard.

*Back-door play*—An offensive move in which a closely guarded player runs away from the basket, then suddenly reverses direction to receive the pass.

*Balanced offense*—A system of scoring plays that puts some offensive team members in good shooting positions and others in good rebounding positions in case shots are missed.

*Bank shot*—A shot, usually taken from an angle, that bounces against the backboard just above the rim and falls into the basket.

*Baseline*—The line and the floor area from sideline to sideline under each basket.

*Blind pass*—A pass to a teammate made by a player who is looking in another direction.

*Blocking*—An illegal play that slows down the progress of an opponent.

*Blocking out*—A defensive move to keep the offensive players away from the basket after a missed shot so the defense can grab the rebound.

*Bomb*—A long shot at the basket, usually a set shot taken by a guard.

*Box-and-one defense*—Four defensive players play a box-shaped zone to get the ball by intercepting passes. The remaining defensive player plays man-to-man defense, guarding the other team's best shooter.

*Boxer's shuffle*—A sliding step used by defensive players for moving quickly in any direction.

*Burning the nets*—A phrase used when a player makes basket after basket without missing.

*Chaser*—The front player in a zone defense whose duty is to force the other team to make bad passes.

*Check-off*—A defensive move in which two players quickly swap the players they are supposed to be guarding.

*Clear-out*—Four offensive players moving to one side of the playing court to allow their remaining teammate room to make a solo play.

*Clogging the middle*—A defensive team maneuver in which the players gather in front of the other team's basket forcing the offensive players to take long shots rather than lay-ups.

*Crash the boards*—Grabbing the ball after a teammate has missed a shot to get a second and third shot at the basket.

*Crossover dribble*—Changing the direction of a player's dribble to confuse the defensive player nearest him.

*Cutting*—Moving quickly toward the basket to receive a pass from a teammate.

*Dead ball*—The ball when not in play.

*Double dribble*—Dribbling again after having already stopped.

*Double pivot*—An offensive play using two centers or pivot players.

*Double screen*—Two offensive players standing close together in front of a teammate who is taking a clear shot.

*Double-team*—Two offensive players guarding one offensive man.

*Down the middle*—An offensive play in which a player runs or dribbles down the foul lane toward the basket.

*Driving lay-up*—A twisting, spinning lay-up shot following a driving dribble to the basket.

*Fakes and feints*—Tricky moves of the eyes, head, and/or body used to throw an opponent off balance.

*Fast break*—A combination of quick passes and lane running used to move the ball downcourt toward the basket before the other team can get there to prevent a play.

*Field goal*—A successful two-point shot, but not a free throw.

*Floating*—Guarding an offensive player while in position to help teammates with their guarding, if necessary.

*Follow-through*—Extension of the arms toward the flight of the ball after passing or shooting.

*Foul*—An infraction or breaking of the rules—usually illegal physical contact—for which a penalty is charged.

*Free throw*—A one-point free shot given to a player because of a foul by the opposing team.

*Free-throw lane*—The area inside the large rectangle under each basket.

*Free-throw line*—A floor line fifteen feet in front of each basket, behind which players must stand to shoot free throws.

*Freeze*—To keep possession of the ball until time runs out.

*Full-court press*—A defensive mode in which the defensive players guard the other team very closely all over the court.

*Give-and-go*—An offensive play in which one player gives the ball to a teammate and then runs to the basket for a return pass.

*Goaltending*—To illegally block a shot after the ball has started to come down into the basket.

*Jab-stepping*—A fake in which the player with the ball steps quickly toward the basket throwing his defender off balance to get free for a shot.

*Key*—Semi-circular court marking behind the foul line in front of the basket.

*Lay-up*—A shot at the basket from directly underneath it.

*Leg-hooking*—Offensive move in which a closely guarded player stretches one leg to the side of the defensive player and steps quickly around him.

*Man-to-man*—A defensive system in which each player guards a specific player on the opposing team.

*Off-the-ball foul*—A foul committed by a player or players not near the ball.

*Outlet pass*—The first pass of a fast break.

*Pick*—A legal block of a running defensive player by

an offensive man, who stands still to make contact.

*Pick-and-roll*—An offensive play in which one player makes a pick, hands the ball off to a teammate, then heads for the basket to receive a pass.

*Pivoting*—Making a turn on one foot while keeping it in contact with the floor.

*Pivot player*—Another term for center.

*Playmaker*—A player, usually a guard, who starts off all offensive plays; sometimes called the team "quarterback."

*Post player*—A tall player, usually the center, who takes an offensive position on one side of the free throw lane or at the free throw line.

*Rebounding*—Getting the ball after a missed shot.

*Roll*—Cutting quickly to the basket after making a pick.

*Set play*—A prearranged offensive play.

*Set shot*—When a player stops, takes aim, and "gets set" before shooting the ball.

*Stagger stance*—The position an individual defensive player takes while guarding, in which his feet are spread and his body is bent over slightly.

*Strong side*—The side of the playing court where the ball is being handled.

*Submarining*—A foul in which one player runs under a player who has jumped high into the air, causing the player to fall.

*Sweep the boards*—To jump higher than all other players and grab a rebound.

*Switch*—When two players exchange their opponents during the time they are guarding.

*Telegraphing*—When an offensive player makes it obvious to others where he is going to pass the ball by raising his arm in a passing motion or looking too long at a teammate.

*Three-second rule*—Makes it illegal for an offensive player to remain in the free-throw lane three seconds or more.

*Tip-in*—A rebound that is tapped into the basket rather than grabbed and tossed to another player.

*Trailer*—The fourth player downcourt on a fast break.

*Trap*—Double-teaming a player who has the ball.

*Traveling*—Running or walking while holding the ball.

*Turnovers*—Errors that cause the offensive team to lose possession of the ball.

*Violations*—Infractions of the rules, such as traveling and three-seconds-in-the-lane, that result in loss of the ball rather than in free throws.

*Weak side*—The side of the playing court where the ball is *not* being handled.

*Zone defense*—Each defensive player guards an area of the court rather than an individual player.

Follow Jefferson High's star center, Brian Davis, as he looks to a former star turned dropout for some pointers on tough city ball in the next action-packed book:


HOOPS #2: Long-Shot Center